PENGUIN CLASSICS
Liberty Bar

'I love reading Simenon. He makes me think of Chekhov'
– William Faulkner

'A truly wonderful writer . . . marvellously readable – lucid, simple, absolutely in tune with the world he creates'
– Muriel Spark

'Few writers have ever conveyed with such a sure touch, the bleakness of human life'
– A. N. Wilson

'One of the greatest writers of the twentieth century . . . Simenon was unequalled at making us look inside, though the ability was masked by his brilliance at absorbing us obsessively in his stories'
– *Guardian*

'A novelist who entered his fictional world as if he were part of it'
– Peter Ackroyd

'The greatest of all, the most genuine novelist we have had in literature'
– André Gide

'Superb . . . The most addictive of writers . . . A unique teller of tales'
– *Observer*

'The mysteries of the human personality are revealed in all their disconcerting complexity'
– Anita Brookner

'A writer who, more than any other crime novelist, combined a high literary reputation with popular appeal'
– P. D. James

'A supreme writer . . . Unforgettable vividness'
– *Independent*

'Compelling, remorseless, brilliant'
– John Gray

'Extraordinary masterpieces of the twentieth century'
– John Banville

GEORGES SIMENON

Liberty Bar

Translated by DAVID WATSON

PENGUIN BOOKS

PENGUIN BOOKS

UK | USA | Canada | Ireland | Australia
India | New Zealand | South Africa

Penguin Books is part of the Penguin Random House group of companies
whose addresses can be found at global.penguinrandomhouse.com.

First published in French as *Liberty Bar* by Fayard 1932
This translation first published in Penguin Books 2015
002

Set in Dante MT Std 12.5/15pt
Typeset by Palimpsest Book Production Limited, Falkirk, Stirlingshire
Printed in Great Britain by Clays Ltd, St Ives plc

A CIP catalogue record for this book is available from the British Library

ISBN: 978-0-141-39609-5

www.greenpenguin.co.uk

MIX
Paper from
responsible sources
FSC® C018179

Penguin Random House is committed to a
sustainable future for our business, our readers
and our planet. This book is made from Forest
Stewardship Council® certified paper.

1. The Dead Man and His Two Women

It all began with a holiday feeling. When Maigret stepped off the train, half of the railway station at Antibes was bathed in sunlight so intense that the people coming and going were reduced to shadows. Shadows in straw hats and white trousers, carrying tennis racquets. The air was humming. There were palm trees and cactuses along the quayside, a strip of blue sea beyond the street-lamps.

Someone was running to meet him.

'Detective Chief Inspector Maigret, I believe? I recognized you from a photo that was in the papers . . . Inspector Boutigues . . .'

Boutigues! Even the name was comical! Boutigues had already picked up Maigret's suitcases and was dragging them towards the subway. He was wearing a pearl-grey suit with a red carnation in his buttonhole and shoes with fabric uppers.

'Is this your first visit to Antibes?'

Maigret mopped his brow and tried to keep up with his cicerone as he threaded his way between the groups of people, overtaking everyone. Eventually, he found himself standing before a horse-drawn carriage with a cream-coloured canvas roof, its small tassels bobbing about. Another forgotten sensation: the bounce of the springs, the coachman's crack of the whip, the muffled sound of hoofs on softened bitumen.

'We'll go and have a drink first . . . No, no, I insist . . . The Café Glacier, coachman . . .'

It was nearby. Boutigues explained:

'Place Macé . . . In the centre of Antibes . . .'

A pretty square with a garden, and cream or orange canopies on all the houses. They simply had to sit out on a terrace and drink a Pernod. Opposite was a shop window full of sports outfits, swimming-costumes, beach robes . . . To the left, a photographer's studio . . . A few smart cars parked along the pavement . . . That holiday feeling again!

'Would you like to see the prisoners first or visit the scene of the crime?'

And Maigret replied without really knowing what he was saying, as if someone had asked him what he was drinking:

'The crime scene.'

The holiday continued. Maigret smoked a cigar that his colleague had offered him. The horse trotted along the promenade. To the right, villas hidden away among the pines; to the left, a few rocks, then the blue of the sea dotted here and there with white sails.

'Have you got your bearings yet? Behind us is Antibes . . . Where we are is the start of Cap d'Antibes, which is nothing but villas, some very expensive villas at that . . .'

Maigret nodded, blissfully. His head was befuddled by all this sunshine, and he squinted at Boutigues' red flower.

'Boutigues, wasn't it?'

'Yes, I'm a Niçois. Or rather, I'm Nicene . . .'

In other words, pure Niçois, Niçois squared, cubed!

'Over here. Can you see that white villa? That one there.'

It wasn't intentional, but Maigret observed all this in disbelief. He just couldn't get into work mode, couldn't convince himself that he was here to investigate a crime.

He had, however, received some very particular instructions:

'A man called Brown has been killed in Cap d'Antibes. It's all over the papers. Best if you avoid any dramas.'

'Understood.'

'During the war, Brown worked for military intelligence.'

'Ditto.'

And here they were. The carriage drew to a halt. Boutigues took a small key from his pocket and opened the gate, then crunched along the gravel of the path.

'It's one of the least attractive villas on the cape!'

However, it wasn't that bad either. The mimosas filled the air with a sickly scent. There were still a few golden oranges hanging on the miniature trees. Then there were some odd-looking flowers that Maigret didn't even know.

'The property opposite belongs to a maharajah . . . He's probably in residence right now . . . Five hundred metres further along, on the left, there is a member of the Academy . . . Then there is that famous dancer who lives with an English lord . . .'

Yes! And so what? Maigret wanted to settle down on the bench next to the house and sleep for an hour. He had, after all, been travelling all night.

'I'll fill you in on the bare bones of the situation.'

Boutigues had opened the door, and they found themselves in a cool hallway whose picture windows looked out over the sea.

'Brown lived here for about ten years . . .'

'Did he work?'

'No . . . he must have had a private income . . . People used to call them Brown and his two women . . .'

'Two?'

'Only one of them was actually his mistress: the daughter . . . Her name is Gina Martini.'

'She's in prison?'

'Her mother too . . . The three of them lived together without a maid . . .'

That much was evident from the state of the house, which was far from clean. There were maybe one or two beautiful things, some valuable items of furniture, some objects that had seen better days.

Everything was dirty and in a mess. There were too many rugs, hangings and throws spread out over the armchairs, too many things impregnated with dust . . .

'These are the facts: Brown had a garage just next to the villa . . . He kept an old-fashioned car which he drove himself . . . He used it mainly to get to the market in Antibes . . .'

'Yes,' sighed Maigret, as he watched a man fishing for sea-urchins, probing the bed of the clear sea with his split reed.

'Someone noticed that the car had been left by the roadside for three days and nights . . . The people around here don't poke their noses into each other's business . . . No one was unduly worried . . . On Monday . . .'

'Really? And today's Thursday? . . . OK.'

'On Monday evening, the butcher was driving back from his rounds when he saw the car pull away . . . You'll see his statement later . . . He saw it from behind . . . At first he thought Brown must be drunk, as he was swerving around so much . . . Then the car drove in a straight line . . . So straight a line, in fact, that it crashed into a rock about three hundred metres down the road . . . Before the butcher could intervene, two women got out and, hearing the sound of his engine, started running towards the town . . .'

'Were they carrying baggage?'

'Three suitcases . . . It was dusk . . . The butcher didn't know what to do . . . He came to Place Macé, where, as you can see, there is a police officer on duty . . . The officer set off to look for the two women, and in the end he found them not heading for the station at Antibes, but rather the one at Golfe-Juan, three kilometres away . . .'

'Still carrying the three cases?'

'They'd left one behind along the way. It was discovered yesterday in a tamarisk wood . . . They were a bit flustered . . . They said they were on their way to see a sick relative in Lyon . . . The officer was smart enough to open the cases and inside he found a batch of bearer bonds, a few hundred-pound notes and a number of other objects . . . A crowd had gathered by now . . . It was aperitif time . . . Everyone was out and about, and they escorted the two women to the police station and then on to the prison . . .'

'Did you search the villa?'

'First thing the next morning. We didn't find anything at first. The two women claimed to know nothing about what had happened to Brown. Finally, around midday, a gardener noticed some earth that had been disturbed. Buried under a layer of soil less than five centimetres deep we discovered Brown's body, still fully dressed.'

'And the two women?'

'They changed their tune. They claimed that they had seen the car pull up three days earlier and that they were surprised that Brown hadn't parked it in the garage . . . He staggered across the garden . . . Gina swore at him through the window, thinking he was drunk . . . He fell on the front steps . . .'

'Dead, of course!'

'As dead as can be! He had been stabbed from behind, right between the shoulder-blades.'

'And they kept him in the house for three days?'

'Yes! And they couldn't provide a plausible explanation! They claimed that Brown had a horror of the police and the like . . .

'They buried him and made off with the money and the most valuable objects! . . . I can understand the car being parked on the road for three days . . . Gina was not a good driver, and she was nervous about backing it into the garage . . . But here's a thing – do you think there was blood inside the car?

'Not a drop! They swear that they cleaned it all up . . .'

'Is that all?'

'That's all! They were furious! They asked us to let them go . . .'

The horse whinnied outside. Maigret couldn't smoke his cigar to the end but didn't dare throw it away.

'A whisky?' suggested Boutigues, spotting a drinks cabinet.

It all seemed terribly undramatic. Maigret was trying in vain to take it all seriously. Was it because of the sun, the mimosas, the oranges, the fisherman looking for sea-urchins in three metres of limpid water?

'Could you give me the keys to the house?'

'Of course! Once you take on the case officially . . .'

Maigret drained the glass of whisky that was offered to him, looked at the record on the gramophone, fiddled with the buttons on a wireless. A voice emerged:

'. . . fully grown wheat . . . November . . .'

At that moment he noticed a portrait hanging behind the radio set, which he took down to inspect more closely.

'Is that him?'

'Yes! I've never seen him alive, but I recognize him . . .'

Maigret switched the wireless off with a hint of nervous excitation. Something had been sparked inside him. Interest? More than that!

A confused feeling, and not a pleasant one. Up to that point, Brown had just been Brown, a stranger, almost certainly a foreigner, who had died in somewhat mysterious circumstances. No one had taken an interest in his thoughts and emotions when he was alive, or wondered what he had suffered . . . And now, looking at the portrait, Maigret was troubled, because he felt as if he knew this man . . . Although not in the sense of having seen him before . . .

No! He wasn't concerned about his features . . . The

broad face of a man in good, indeed robust, health, with thinning red hair, a pencil moustache, large, clear eyes . . .

But there was something about his general bearing, his expression, that reminded Maigret of himself. That way of holding the shoulders slightly pulled in . . . That exaggeratedly calm gaze . . . That good-natured but ironic curl of the lips . . . This wasn't Brown the corpse . . . He was someone that the inspector wanted to know and who intrigued him.

'Another whisky? It's not bad . . .'

Boutigues was enjoying himself! He was astonished when Maigret didn't respond to his quips but continued to look around him with an absent air.

'Shall we offer the coachman one?'

'No! Let's go . . .'

'You're not going to inspect the house?'

'Another time!'

Oh, to be alone! Not to have his head buzzing with the sunshine. As they returned to town, he didn't speak, and only acknowledged Boutigues' remarks with a nod of the head. The latter wondered what he had done to deserve this treatment from his companion.

'You'll see the old town . . . The prison is right next to the market . . . Morning's the best time . . .'

'Which hotel?' the coachman asked, turning round.

'Do you want one right in the centre?' Boutigues asked.

'Drop me here! I'll sort it out . . .'

There was a small family-run pension-style hotel halfway between the Cap and the town.

'Are you not coming to the prison this evening?'

'Tomorrow, I'll see . . .'

'Want me to come and pick you up? By the way, if you fancy going to the casino at Juan-les-Pins after dinner, I'll . . .'

'No, thank you. I'm tired.'

He wasn't tired. But he wasn't in good form. He felt hot. He was sweaty. In his room, which looked out to sea, he poured some water into the bath, then changed his mind and went outside, with his pipe between his teeth and his hands in his pockets. He caught a glimpse of the small white tables in the dining room, the napkins displayed like fans in the glasses, the bottles of wine and mineral water, the maid sweeping up . . .

'Brown was killed by a knife in the back, and his two women tried to escape with the money . . .'

But this was all rather vague. And, in spite of himself, he looked at the sun, which was slowly sinking into the sea, picking out the thin white line of the Promenade des Anglais in Nice.

Then he stared at the mountains, whose summits were still white with snow.

'In other words, Nice to the left, twenty-five kilometres, Cannes to the right, twelve kilometres . . . The mountains behind and the sea in front.'

He was already constructing a world centred on the villa of Brown and his women.

A world sticky with sunshine, the scent of mimosas and sickly sweet flowers, drunken flies, cars gliding over softened asphalt . . .

He didn't have the strength to walk into the centre of

Antibes, just a kilometre away. He went back inside his hotel, the Hôtel Bacon, and phoned the prison and asked to speak to the governor.

'The governor is on holiday.'

'His deputy?'

'He doesn't have one. There's just me here.'

'All right, then! Have the two prisoners brought to the villa in one hour's time.'

The warder on the other end of the line must have caught the sun himself. Perhaps had a Pernod or two. He forgot to ask Maigret for his credentials.

'OK, will you return them to us?'

And Maigret yawned, stretched, filled another pipe. But this pipe did not have the usual flavour.

'Brown was killed, and the two women . . .'

He set off on foot, walking slowly, towards the villa. He passed the spot where the car had hit the rock. He almost laughed. For it was precisely the sort of accident that happened to novice drivers. A few zigzags before straightening up . . . Then, having achieved a straight line, finding it impossible to turn . . .

The butcher appearing behind them in the semi-dark . . . The two women starting to run with their too-heavy suitcases, abandoning one by the roadside . . .

A limousine drove past, driven by a chauffeur. An Asian face in the back: no doubt the maharajah . . . The sea was red and blue, with a hint of orange in between . . . The electric lights were coming on, still pale . . .

Maigret was all alone in this huge panorama. He went up to the gate of the villa, like an owner returning home, turned the key in the lock, left the gate open and ascended the front steps. The trees were full of birds. The door creaked – a sound that Brown must have been familiar with.

On the threshold, Maigret tried to analyse the smell . . . Every house has its own smell . . . This one was based on a strong perfume, probably musk . . . Then the odour of stale cigars . . .

He switched on the electric light, then went to the living room and sat down next to the wireless and the record-player, in the seat where Brown must have sat, as it was the most worn chair.

'He was murdered, and the two women . . .'

The light was bad, but he spotted a standard lamp which was plugged into an electric socket. It was covered by an enormous lampshade made of pink silk. When he turned on the lamp, the room came to life.

'During the war, he worked for military intelligence . . .'

That was well known. That is why the local papers, which he had read on the train, were making such a big deal out of it. The public loved the glamour and mystery of espionage.

Hence the idiotic headlines such as:

AN INTERNATIONAL AFFAIR

A SECOND KOTIOPOV AFFAIR?

A SPY DRAMA

Some journalists saw the hand of the Cheka, others the workings of the Secret Service.

Maigret looked around and had the feeling that there was something missing. And he located it. What was creating the chill was a large picture window, behind which the night was turning stale. There was a curtain, so he closed it.

'There! A woman in this armchair, probably with a piece of sewing . . .'

And there it was: a piece of embroidery, on a small table.

'The other one in this corner . . .'

And in the corner there was a book: *The Passions of Rudolf Valentino* . . .

'All that is missing is Gina and her mother . . .'

He had to stare hard to make out the gentle wash of the water along the rocks of the coastline. Maigret looked at the portrait again, which bore the signature of a photographer in Nice.

'No dramas!'

In other words, discover the truth as quickly as possible to cut short the gossip of the press and public. There were steps on the gravel in the garden. A bell with a very serious, very seductive ring sounded in the hall. Maigret went to the door and could make out the figure of a man in a kepi next to two female silhouettes.

'You can go . . . I'll take charge of them . . . Come in, ladies!'

He appeared to be receiving them. He couldn't make out their features yet. On the other hand, he caught a strong scent of musk.

'I hope you believe us now . . .' came a rather strained voice.

'Of course! . . . Come in, then . . . Make yourselves comfortable.'

They entered into the light. The mother had a very lined face, plastered with a thick layer of make-up. She stood in the middle of the living room and looked around her, as if checking that nothing was missing.

The other one was more suspicious; she observed Maigret, smoothed the folds of her dress and attempted a smile that she intended to be alluring.

'Is it true that they have brought you down from Paris especially?'

'Please, take your coats off . . . Make yourselves at home . . .'

They still didn't understand what was going on. It was as if they were strangers in their own house. They feared a trap.

'We're going to have a bit of a chat, the three of us . . .'

'Do you know something?'

It was the girl who had spoken. The mother said sharply: 'Be careful, Gina!'

In truth, Maigret was once again having great difficulty taking his role seriously. The older woman, despite her make-up, was a ghastly sight.

As for the girl, with her full, almost too buxom figure squeezed into a dress of dark silk, she was a classic pseudo femme fatale.

And the smell! That musky odour that once more permeated the atmosphere of the room!

It evoked a concierge's lodge in a small theatre.

Nothing dramatic, nothing mysterious. The mother

doing her embroidery and keeping an eye on her daughter. And the girl reading the adventures of Valentino!

Maigret, who had returned to his seat in Brown's armchair, watched them both with expressionless eyes but was puzzled:

'How on earth did a fellow like Brown spend ten years with these two women?'

Ten years! Long days of unbroken sunshine, the scent of mimosa, with the constant swell of the immense blue sea beneath their windows, and ten years of quiet, interminable evenings, barely disturbed by the murmur of waves on the shore, and the two women, the mother in her armchair, the girl next to the lamp with the pink silk lampshade . . .

He mechanically played with the photo of this Brown, who had the impertinence to resemble him.

2. Tell Me About Brown . . .

'What did he do in the evening?'

And Maigret, sitting with his legs crossed, looked on, bored, as the old woman displayed all her airs and graces.

'We rarely went out . . . Mostly, my daughter read while . . .'

'Tell me about Brown!'

Somewhat ruffled, she let slip:

'He didn't do anything!'

'He listened to the wireless,' sighed Gina, who had adopted a nonchalant pose. 'As much as I like real music, I hate . . .'

'Tell me about Brown. Was he in good health?'

'If he'd listened to me he wouldn't have had all that trouble with his liver, or his kidneys . . . Once a man gets past forty . . .'

Maigret had the expression of someone listening to an idiotic comedian telling old jokes and roaring with laughter at every punchline. Each of the women was as ridiculous as the other, the mother with her nose in the air, the daughter posing like a rosy-cheeked odalisque.

'You said that he came home that evening in the car, walked across the garden and fell on the front steps.'

'As if he were dead drunk, yes! I yelled at him through the window that he couldn't come in until he had sobered up.'

'Did he often come home drunk?'

The old woman again:

'If only you knew how much he has tested our patience, during these last ten years . . .'

'Did he often come home drunk?'

'Every time he went on one of his little escapades or almost every time . . . We called them his novenas . . .'

'And did he do these novenas often?'

Maigret couldn't resist a happy smile. So Brown hadn't spent every day in the last ten years in the company of the two women!

'About once a month.'

'And for how long?'

'He was away for three or four days, sometimes more . . . He would come home filthy, stinking of alcohol . . .'

'And yet you still let him go?'

A silence. The old woman stiffened and shot the inspector a sharp look.

'I'm guessing that, between you, you must have exerted some influence over him?'

'He had to go to fetch some money!'

'And you couldn't go with him?'

Gina had stood up. She sighed wearily:

'This is all quite trying! . . . I'll be honest with you, inspector . . . We weren't married, even though William always treated me as his wife and even had my mother move in with us . . . As far as people were concerned I was Madame Brown . . . Otherwise, I wouldn't have put up with it . . .'

'Me neither!' her mother piped up.

'But it's all a bit more complicated than that . . . I won't speak ill of William . . . But there was just one point on which we differed: money . . .'

'Was he rich?'

'I don't know . . .'

'And you don't know where his fortune came from? . . . Is that why you let him leave each month, to go in search of cash . . . ?'

'I tried to follow him, I admit . . . I had a right to, didn't I? . . . But he was very careful . . . He always took the car . . .'

Maigret was feeling relaxed now. He was even starting to enjoy himself. He had made his peace with this joker called Brown who lived with two shrews, from whom, over the course of ten years, he had managed to conceal the source of his income.

'Did he bring home large amounts of cash at a time?'

'Barely enough to live off for a month . . . Two thousand francs . . . In the second half of the month we had to tighten our belts . . .'

He had hit a nerve! Just the thought of it was enough to send them both into a rage!

Indeed! Once the funds started to run low, they must have watched William anxiously, wondering whether he was intending to go on a novena again. They could scarcely say to him: 'So . . . Are you not going off on one of your sprees?'

They had to be more oblique! Maigret could see that clearly!

'So who held the purse strings?'

'Mother,' said Gina.

'Did she plan your meals?'

'Of course! And she did the cooking! Since we didn't have enough money to hire a servant!'

So that was the key to it. At the end of the month, they started serving Brown meagre, inedible meals. And when he made a fuss, they replied: 'That's all we can manage on the money we have left!'

Did he need much persuading? Or, on the contrary, was he eager to go?

'At what time of day did he usually set off?'

'No particular time! You'd think he was out in the garden, or else pottering in the garage, cleaning the car . . . Then all of a sudden you'd hear the car engine . . .'

'And you tried to follow him . . . In a taxi?'

'I had one parked a hundred metres from here for three days . . . But he managed to shake us off in the backstreets of Antibes . . . However, I do know where he parked the car – in a garage in Cannes. He left it there the whole time when he was on one of his escapades . . .'

'So he could have taken the train to Paris or anywhere?'

'Maybe!'

'Or maybe he stayed in the area?'

'It would be surprising that no one ever bumped into him . . .'

'Was he returning from a novena the day that he died?'

'Yes . . . He'd been away for seven days . . .'

'Did you find any money on him?'

'Two thousand francs, as usual.'

'Do you want to know what I think?' the old woman interjected. 'Well, I think William must have had a much bigger income . . . Maybe four thousand . . . Maybe five . . . He preferred to spend the rest of it himself . . . And he condemned us to live off a paltry sum . . .'

Maigret was blissfully ensconced in Brown's armchair. The more the interrogation proceeded, the wider his smile grew.

'Was he mean?'

'Him? . . . He was the finest of men . . .'

'Just a moment. If you'll bear with me, I'd like to reconstruct the timetable of a typical day. Who would get up first?'

'William . . . He would mostly sleep on the divan in the hall. We'd hear him moving around at the crack of dawn . . . I told him a hundred times . . .'

'Excuse me, did he make the coffee?'

'Yes . . . When we came down, around ten, there would be coffee on the stove . . . But it was cold . . .'

'And Brown?'

'He would be pottering in the garden or in the garage. Or else he would sit by the sea. Come market day, he would get the car out . . . Another thing I could never get him to do: wash before going out shopping. He would always have his nightshirt on under his jacket, his slippers, his hair in a mess . . . We would go into Antibes. He would wait outside the shops . . .'

'Did he get dressed when he got home?'

'Sometimes yes! Sometimes no! He could sometimes go four or five days without washing.'

'Where did you eat?'

'In the kitchen. When you don't have a maid, you try not to get all the rooms dirty . . .'

'And in the afternoon?'

Good heavens! They had a siesta. Then, at around five o'clock, he would mope around the house in his slippers again.

'Lots of arguments?'

'Almost none! Though when you said anything to him, William had an insulting way of snubbing you.'

Maigret did not laugh. He was starting to develop a strong fellow feeling with this confounded Brown.

'So, he was killed . . . That could have happened while he was crossing the garden . . . However, as you found some blood in the car . . .'

'Why would we lie about it?'

'Quite! So, he was killed somewhere else. Or rather, wounded! And, instead of taking himself to a doctor, or to the police station, he came here to expire . . . Did you carry the body indoors?'

'We couldn't leave it outside!'

'Now, tell me why you did not inform the authorities . . . I'm sure you must have had an excellent reason . . .'

The old woman stood up straight and insisted:

'Yes, inspector! And I will explain that reason to you! You would have found out the truth one day in any case. Brown had married before, in Australia . . . He is an Australian . . . His wife is still alive. She has always refused to divorce him, who knows why? If we don't live in the finest villa on the Côte d'Azur, it's all because of her . . .'

'Have you ever seen her?'

'She has never left Australia . . . But she has arranged things so that her husband was placed under legal guardianship . . . For ten years we have been living with him, taking care of him, consoling him . . . Thanks to us he has a bit of money put aside . . . So, if . . .'

'If Madame Brown had learned about her husband's death, she would have had all his assets here seized!'

'Exactly! We would have made all those sacrifices for nothing! And not just that. I am not entirely without resources of my own. My husband was in the army, and I still draw a small pension . . . A lot of the things here belong to me . . . But this woman has the law on her side and she could simply have turned us out of our house . . .'

'So you hesitated . . . You weighed up the pros and cons for three days, with the dead body presumably lying on the divan in the hall . . .'

'Two days! We buried him on the second day . . .'

'The pair of you! Then you gathered up the most valuable items in the house and . . . So tell me, where did you intend to go?'

'Anywhere! Brussels, London . . .'

'Had you driven the car before?' Maigret asked Gina.

'Never! Though I have started it up in the garage.'

A heroic undertaking, then! It was almost like a dream, this departure, with the dead body in the garden, the three heavy suitcases and the car swerving all over the place . . .

Maigret was starting to feel sick of the atmosphere in here, the smell of musk, the reddish light filtering through the lampshade.

'Do you mind if I have a look round the house?'

They had regained their poise, their dignity. Perhaps they even felt a bit baffled because the inspector was taking everything in his stride and seemed, deep down, to find these events perfectly normal.

'Please excuse the mess.'

And what mess! Mess wasn't the word for it. It was something far more sordid! A cross between a den, where animals live in their own stench, among leftover food and excrement, and a bourgeois interior, with all its preening pomposity.

On a coat-peg in the hall there was an old overcoat that had belonged to William Brown. Maigret searched through its pockets, took out a worn pair of gloves, a key, a tin of cachous.

'He ate cachou lozenges?'

'When he had been drinking, to disguise the smell on his breath. We wouldn't let him touch whisky . . . The bottle is still hidden away.'

Above the coat-peg there was a stag's head with antlers. And further along, a rattan pedestal table with a silver platter for visitors' cards.

'Was he wearing this coat here?'

'No, his gabardine . . .'

The shutters were closed in the dining room. The room was used as little more than a shed, and Brown must have done some fishing, for there were lobster pots stacked on the floor. Then there was the kitchen, where the big stove had never been lit. The alcohol stove was the one that was used. Next to it stood fifty or sixty empty bottles, which had once contained mineral water.

'The water round here is too hard, and . . .'

The stairs, covered with a threadbare carpet, were held

in place by copper grips. You just had to follow the scent of musk to find Gina's bedroom.

No bathroom, no toilet. Dresses thrown higgledy-piggledy on the bed, which was unmade. It was here that they had sorted through the clothes in order to take only the best ones.

Maigret preferred to avoid the old woman's room.

'We had to leave in such a hurry . . . I am so ashamed to show you the house in such a state.'

'I'll come back and see you later.'

'Are we free?'

'Let's just say you won't be going back to prison . . . At least not for the time being . . . But if you try to leave Antibes . . .'

'We wouldn't dream of it!'

They saw him to the door. The old woman remembered her good manners.

'A cigar, inspector?'

Gina went even further. Always best to keep such an influential man onside.

'You can take the whole box. William won't be smoking them . . .'

You couldn't make it up! Outside, Maigret felt almost giddy. He wanted to laugh and grit his teeth at the same time. Once outside the gate, he turned around and got quite a different view of the villa, stark white against the greenery.

The moon was just at the angle of the roof. To the right, the shiny sea, the quivering mimosas . . .

He had his gabardine under his arm. He walked back to

the Hôtel Bacon without thinking, just vague images running through his head, some of them painful, some comic.

'Good old William!'

It was late. The dining room was empty apart from a serving girl who was reading the paper. That was when he noticed that it wasn't his gabardine he had brought with him, but Brown's – filthy and stained with oil and grease.

In the left pocket there was a monkey wrench, in the right a handful of change and a few small square coins made of copper and marked with a figure. They were tokens for fruit machines to be found on the counters of small bars.

There were about ten of them.

'Hello! Inspector Boutigues here. Do you want me to pick you up from your hotel?'

It was nine in the morning. Maigret had opened his window and been dozing for six hours on and off, luxuriating in the knowledge that the Mediterranean was spread out before him.

'To do what?'

'Don't you want to see the body?'

'Yes . . . No . . . Maybe this afternoon . . . Ring me at lunchtime.'

He needed to wake up. In the light of morning, the events of the previous day no longer seemed real. The memory of the two women was more like a half-forgotten nightmare.

They wouldn't be up yet! And if Brown had survived, he would be busy pottering in his garden or garage. All alone. Unwashed. With a pot of cold coffee sitting on an unlit stove.

As he was shaving, Maigret noticed the tokens on the mantelpiece. He had to make an effort to remember what part they played in the story.

'Brown went off on his novena and got killed, either before getting back into his car or inside it, or while crossing the garden, or in the house . . .'

He had already shaved the soap off his left cheek when he murmured:

'Brown can't have gone to any of the small bars in Antibes . . . I'd have heard about it.'

And besides, didn't Gina discover that he parked his car in Cannes? A quarter of an hour later, he was on the phone to the Cannes police.

'Detective Chief Inspector Maigret, Police Judiciaire . . . Could you provide me with a list of bars with fruit machines?'

'There aren't any now. They were banned two months ago by order of the Prefect. You won't find any anywhere on the Côte d'Azur . . .'

He asked his landlady where he could find a taxi.

'Going where?'

'Cannes!'

'Then you don't need a taxi. There's a very regular bus service, leaving from Place Macé.'

And so there was. In the morning sun Place Macé was even more colourful than on the previous evening. Brown must have passed through it when he drove his two women to the market.

Maigret took the bus. Half an hour later, he was in Cannes, where he went to the garage that he had been told about. It was near the Croisette. White everywhere! Huge white hotels, white shops, white trousers and dresses, white sails out at sea.

It was as if life were no more than a pantomime fairy-tale, a white and blue fairy-tale.

'Is this where Monsieur Brown left his car?'

'Here we go!'

'Here we go what?'

'I'm going to be given a hard time over this! I knew this was coming when I heard he'd been killed . . . Yes, it was here. I've got nothing to hide. He'd drop his car off here in the evening, then he'd come to pick it up eight, nine, ten days later . . .'

'Drunk?'

'Every time I saw him, yes!'

'Do you know where he went afterwards?'

'When? After he parked the car? No idea.'

'Did he ask you to clean it, give it a once-over?'

'No, never! He hadn't even changed the oil for a year.'

'What did you make of him?'

The garage owner shrugged his shoulders.

'Nothing.'

'Bit of an eccentric?'

'The Côte d'Azur's full of them. You get used to them. Scarcely notice them any more! Look, just yesterday this American girl comes by and wants me to do her a chassis in the shape of a swan . . . I thought: sure, if you're willing to pay!'

26

There were still the fruit machines to follow up on. Maigret went into a bar near the harbour, which was full of nothing but yachtsmen.

'Do you have any fruit machines?'

'They were banned a month ago . . . But we've got a new type of machine. In two or three months they'll ban them too . . .'

'So there are no machines anywhere else?'

The proprietor was non-committal on that one.

'What will you have?'

Maigret had a vermouth. He looked at the yachts lined up in the harbour, then the sailors, who had the names of their boats embroidered on to their jerseys.

'Do you know Brown?'

'Which Brown? . . . The one who got killed? . . . He didn't come here.'

'Where did he go?'

A vague shrug. The proprietor had other customers to serve. It was getting warmer. Even though it was only March, Maigret was sweating, a smell of summer.

'I've heard people talk about him, but I can't remember who,' the proprietor said as he came back, bottle in hand.

'Too bad! What I'm looking for is a fruit machine . . .'

Brown took his raincoat with him during his novenas. So it was very likely that, on his return, the two women searched through his pockets.

Therefore the tokens dated from his final trip . . .

But this was all rather vague and insubstantial. And there was this sun which filled Maigret with a desire to sit on a terrace, like everyone else, and watch the boats barely moving on a calm sea.

Bright trams . . . beautiful cars . . . He found the town's shopping street, parallel to the Croisette . . .

'If Brown spent his novenas in Cannes,' he grumbled, 'it wasn't round here.'

He walked. He stopped now and then to go into a bar. He drank vermouth and talked fruit machines.

'It goes in waves. They raid us every three months. Then we get some new ones and carry on as normal until the next time . . .'

'Do you know Brown?'

'The Brown who was killed?'

It was monotonous. It was past noon. The sun was beating down on the streets. Maigret wanted to accost a policeman like a tourist out on the town and ask him:

'Where's the party round here?'

If Madame Maigret had been there she would have noticed that he was rather glassy-eyed due to all the vermouths he had drunk.

He turned a corner, then another, and suddenly he wasn't in Cannes any more, with its large white buildings resplendent in the sun, but in another world entirely: narrow alleyways no more than a metre wide with lines of washing strung across from one house to another.

To the right, a sign: 'The Sailors' Rest'.

To the left, a sign: 'Liberty Bar'.

Maigret went into the Sailors' Rest, ordered a vermouth and stood at the counter.

'Hey, I thought you had a fruit machine . . .'

'*Had* one, yes!'

His head felt heavy and his legs were aching from walking all around the town.

'Some places still have them.'

'Some, yes!' muttered the barman as he wiped the counter-top with a towel. 'There are always some who slip through the net. Still, that's none of our business, is it . . .'

And he looked out across the street as he answered Maigret's next question:

'Two francs twenty-five . . . I don't have any change . . .'

So the inspector went across the road to the Liberty Bar.

3. William's Goddaughter

The room, which was empty, was no bigger than two metres by three. You had to go down two steps, as it was below street level.

A narrow bar. A shelf containing a dozen glasses. The fruit machine. And two tables.

At the back, a glass door with a net curtain. Through the curtain the shape of heads moving. But no one got up to greet the customer. Just a woman's voice, shouting:

'What are you waiting for?'

Maigret went in. There was another step to go down, and the window, which was flush with the courtyard, looked like a vent. In the half-light Maigret could make out three people sitting round a table.

The woman who had cried out didn't stop eating but looked at him as he himself had the habit of looking at people: calmly, picking up every detail.

With her elbows on the table, she finally gave a sigh and indicated a footstool with her chin.

'You took your time!'

Next to her sat a man whom Maigret could only see from the back. He was dressed in a very clean sailor's uniform. His fair hair was close cropped on his neck. He was wearing cuffs.

'Carry on eating,' the woman said to him. 'It's nothing . . .'

Finally, at the other end of the table, a third person, a young woman with a lustreless complexion who stared suspiciously at Maigret with her big eyes.

She was wearing a dressing gown. The whole of her left breast was on display, but no one paid it any attention.

'Take a seat. Do you mind if we finish eating?'

How old was she – forty-five, fifty, maybe older? It was hard to tell. She was fat, smiling, sure of herself. You could tell that nothing fazed her, that she had seen it all, heard it all, experienced it all.

One look was enough to tell her what Maigret was here for. She hadn't even stood up. She was cutting thick slices off a leg of mutton, which caught Maigret's attention for a moment, for he had rarely seen one as succulent.

'So are you from Nice or Antibes? I haven't seen you round here before.'

'Police Judiciaire, Paris . . .'

'Ah!'

That 'ah' showed that she understood the difference, recognized her visitor's rank.

'So it's true, then?'

'What?'

'That William was some sort of important person . . .'

Now Maigret could see the sailor in profile. He was no ordinary sailor. His uniform was cut from very fine cloth. He was wearing gold braid, a yacht club badge on his cap.

He seemed put out. He ate without lifting his eyes from his plate.

'Who is this?'

'We call him Yan . . . I don't know his real name . . . He's a steward on board the *Ardena*, a Swedish yacht that winters in Cannes every year . . . Yan is the butler, aren't you, Yan? . . . This gentleman is from the police . . . I told you about William . . .'

Yan nodded his head but showed little sign of having understood.

'He says yes, but he doesn't really know what I'm talking about!' the woman said, paying no attention to the sailor. 'He's never got the hang of French . . . But he's a good guy . . . He has a wife and kids back home . . . Show them your photo, Yan . . . Yes, photo!'

And the man took a photo out of his jacket pocket. It showed a young woman sitting in front of a door with two babies in the grass in front of her.

'Twins!' the woman explained. 'Yan comes here to eat now and again, because it feels like family here. He brought the mutton and the peaches . . .'

Maigret looked at the girl, who was still making no effort to cover her breast.

'And she is . . . ?'

'This is Sylvie, William's goddaughter . . .'

'Goddaughter?'

'Oh, not in the church sense! . . . He wasn't there when she was christened . . . Were you christened, Sylvie?'

'Of course!'

She continued to look at Maigret with suspicion while nibbling away at her food without relish.

'William was fond of her . . . She told him all her troubles . . . He consoled her . . .'

Maigret was sitting on a stool, his elbows on his knees, his chin in his hands. The fat woman was preparing a salad seasoned with garlic that looked like a work of art.

'Have you eaten?'

He lied.

'Yes . . . I . . .'

'Because you should know . . . we're very easy here . . . Isn't that so, Yan? . . . Look at him! He says yes but he doesn't understand a word . . . I love 'em, these Nordic boys!'

She tasted the salad, added a dash of olive oil with a fruity aroma. There was no cloth on the table, which wasn't very clean. There was a staircase in the kitchen which must have led up to another floor. In the corner there was a sewing machine.

The courtyard was filled with sunlight, so much so that the window was a dazzling rectangle and by contrast the interior felt like a cold, gloomy space.

'You can ask me questions . . . Sylvie knows everything . . . and as for Yan . . .'

'Have you had this bar long?'

'Maybe fifteen years . . . I was married to an Englishman, a former acrobat, so we had all the English sailors come here, as well as music-hall performers . . . My husband drowned nine years ago at the regatta . . . He raced for a baroness who has three boats which you probably know . . .'

'And since then?'

'Nothing! I held on to the house . . .'

'Do you get much business?'

'I don't care about that . . . It's mainly friends, like Yan, like William . . . They know that I'm on my own and like company . . . They come and share a bottle or else bring rockfish, a chicken, and I rustle something up . . .'

She topped up the glasses, and noticed that Maigret didn't have anything to drink.

'You should get the inspector a drink, Sylvie.'

Sylvie got up without a word and went to the bar. She was naked under her dressing gown. Her feet were bare in sandals. She brushed against Maigret as she passed without apologizing. While she was at the bar, the other woman murmured:

'Don't mind her . . . She adored William . . . She's taking it very hard.'

'Does she sleep here?'

'Sometimes she does, sometimes she doesn't.'

'What does she do?'

The woman gave Maigret a reproachful look. She seemed to be saying: 'Do you, a detective chief inspector from the Police Judiciaire, need to ask that question?'

She added immediately:

'Oh! She's a quiet girl, not a bad bone in her body . . .'

'Did William know?'

That look again. Had she got Maigret wrong? Did he not understand anything? Did he need everything spelled out?

Yan had finished eating. He was waiting to speak, but she read his thoughts.

'Yes, you can go, Yan . . . Are you coming this evening?'

'If the owners go to the casino.'

He got up, seemed unsure about the traditional niceties. But, as the woman offered him her forehead, he planted a mechanical kiss, blushing because of the presence of Maigret. He met Sylvie on her way back with a drink.

'You're leaving?'

'Yes . . .'

And he kissed her in the same way, offered Maigret a strange salute, made a quick getaway and literally dived into the street while adjusting his cap.

'That boy doesn't like going out on the town like most yacht sailors . . . He'd rather come here . . .'

She too had finished eating now. She made herself comfortable, both elbows on the table.

'Could you pass the coffee, Sylvie?'

You could barely hear any sound from the street. Without that rectangle of light, it would have been impossible to say what hour of the day or night it was.

An alarm clock in the middle of the mantelpiece marked the passage of time.

'So what is it you want to know exactly? . . . Your good health . . . This is some of William's whisky . . .'

'What do people call you?'

'Jaja . . . Or Big Jaja when they want to tease me . . .'

And she looked at her enormous bosom, which was resting on the table.

'Have you known William long?'

Sylvie had returned to her seat, chin resting in her hand, still not taking her eyes off Maigret. The sleeve of her dressing gown trailed in her food.

'I'd say almost for ever. But I only learned his surname a week ago . . . I should tell you that, when my husband was still alive, the Liberty Bar was famous . . . There were always artists here, and they attracted the rich clientele who came to see them . . .

'Especially the yacht owners: almost all of them are party animals, eccentrics . . . I remember seeing William quite a lot at that time, in his white cap, always with friends or pretty women . . .

'These groups liked to drink champagne until the small hours and they'd stand anyone a round . . .

'Then my husband died . . . I closed for a month . . . It was out of season . . . The following winter I had to spend three weeks in hospital with peritonitis.

'Someone took advantage of the situation and opened a bar right on the harbour itself.

'Since then, it's been quiet . . . I don't even try to attract new customers.

'One day, I saw William again, and it was only then that I properly made his acquaintance . . . We got drunk together . . . We swapped stories . . . He slept on the divan, because he couldn't even stand up . . .'

'Was he still wearing a yachtsman's cap?'

'No! He looked very different. He was a maudlin drinker . . . He got into the habit of coming to see me from time to time . . .'

'Did you know where he lived?'

'No. I wasn't going to interrogate him. And he never talked about his personal business . . .'

'Did he stay here long?'

'Three or four days . . . He brought food with him . . . Or else he gave me money to go to the market . . . He said he didn't eat anywhere as well as he did here.'

And Maigret looked at the pink flesh of the mutton, the remains of the scented salad. It looked really tasty.

'Was Sylvie already with you?'

'I should hope not! She is only twenty-one . . .'

'How did you meet her?'

And as Sylvie had an obstinate look on her face, Jaja said to her:

'The inspector knows the score, OK? . . . It was one evening when William was here . . . It was just the two of us in the bar . . . Sylvie came in with some gentlemen she had met who knows where, travelling salesmen or some such. They were already merry. They ordered some drinks . . . As for her, you could see straight away she was new to all this. She wanted to get them away before they got completely drunk . . . She didn't know what she was doing . . . and so the inevitable happened: in the end they got so drunk that they didn't bother with her any more and went off and left her here . . . She was crying . . . She admitted that she had just arrived from Paris for the season and that she didn't even have enough money to pay for a hotel room . . . She slept with me . . . She got into the habit of coming here . . .'

'Basically,' Maigret grumbled, 'everyone who comes in here gets into the same habit . . .'

And the old woman, beaming, replied:

'What can I say? It's the Lord's own house! We're easy-going here. We take each day as it comes . . .'

And she meant it. Her gaze descended slowly to the young woman's bust and she sighed:

'A shame about her health . . . You can still see her ribs . . . William wanted to pay for her to have a month in a sanatorium, but she refused to go . . .'

'Excuse me, did William . . . and her . . .'

It was Sylvie herself who replied, angrily:

'Never! It's not true . . .'

And Big Jaja explained as she sipped her coffee:

'He wasn't that sort of man . . . Especially not with her . . . That's not to say that he didn't occasionally . . .'

'With whom?'

'Women . . . Just women he picked up here and there . . . But it didn't happen often . . . He wasn't that interested . . .'

'What time did he leave you on Friday?'

'Straight after lunch . . . It must have been two o'clock, like today . . .'

'And he didn't say where he was going?'

'He never spoke about that.'

'Was Sylvie here?'

'She left five minutes before him.'

'To go where?' Maigret asked the girl herself.

And she, still suspicious, replied:

'What's it to you?'

'To the harbour? . . . Is that where . . . ?'

'There and other places!'

'Was there anyone else in the bar?'

'No one . . . It was a hot day . . . I had a nap on the chair for an hour.'

Yet William didn't arrive back at Antibes in his car until after five o'clock!

'Did he go to other bars like this one?'

'No, never. Besides, there are no other bars like this one.'

Quite so! Maigret himself, who had only been there for an hour, felt as if he had known it for ever. Maybe because there was nothing personal. Or maybe because of its relaxed, lazy ambience. You couldn't summon up the determination to get up and leave. Time flowed by slowly. The hands of the alarm clock ticked around the pale clock face. And the rectangle of sun at the window slowly faded.

'I read the papers . . . I didn't even know William's sur-name . . . But I recognized the photo . . . We cried, Sylvie and me . . . What on earth was he doing with those two women? . . . In our situation, you shouldn't get involved in things like that, should you? . . . I expected the police to turn up at any time . . . When you came out of the bar across the road, I thought this might be it . . .'

She spoke slowly. She topped up the drinks. She drank her alcohol in small mouthfuls.

'Whoever did it was a nasty piece of work, because men like William are few and far between . . . And I should know!'

'Did he ever talk to you about his past?'

She gave a sigh. Hadn't Maigret got it yet? This was the bar *where nobody talked about the past*!

'All I can tell you is that he was a gentleman. A man who was once very rich, and perhaps still was . . . I don't know . . . He had a yacht, a load of servants.'

'Was he unhappy?'

She sighed again.

'Can't you understand? . . . You've seen Yan . . . Is he unhappy? . . . But it's still not the same thing . . . Am I unhappy? . . . It doesn't mean that we don't have a drink and talk aimlessly and feel a need to cry . . .'

Sylvie gave her a censorious look. Of course, she had only been drinking coffee while Big Jaja was already on her third glass.

'I'm glad you came, because now I can be shot of it . . . Nothing to hide, nothing to reproach myself about . . . Although with the police, you know it's not that simple . . . If it had been the Cannes police, I'm sure they'd have had me locked . . .'

'Was William a big spender?'

Was she exasperated at her inability to make him understand how it was?

'He spent money but he didn't . . . He gave us cash to buy things to eat and drink . . . Sometimes he paid the gas or electricity bill, or else he gave Sylvie a hundred francs to buy some stockings.'

Maigret was hungry. And there was that delicious leg of mutton just a few centimetres from his nostrils. There were two slices lying on the dish. He picked one up with his fingers and ate it as he spoke, as if he too were now one of the regulars.

'Did Sylvie bring her clients back here?'

'No, never! That would have got us closed down . . . There are plenty of hotels in Cannes for that sort of thing!'

Looking Maigret in the eye, she added:

'Do you believe it was his women who . . .'

At the same moment she turned her head away. Sylvie stood up so as to see through the net curtain over the door. The outside door had been opened. Someone walked across the bar, pushed open the other door and stopped, surprised, when he saw a new face.

Sylvie had got up. Jaja, looking a little pink in the cheeks, said to the new arrival:

'Come in! This is the police inspector who is in charge of William's case . . .'

And to Maigret:

'A friend . . . Joseph . . . He's a waiter at the casino.'

That was evident from the white shirt front and the knot of black tie that Joseph wore under a grey suit and his polished shoes.

'I'll come back . . .' he said.

'No, come in!'

He didn't look too sure.

'I just dropped by to say hello . . . I've got a tip for the race . . .'

'You bet on the horses?' Maigret asked, half turning towards the waiter.

'Now and again . . . Sometimes clients give me tips . . . I'd best be off . . .'

And he beat a retreat, though not before Maigret got the impression that he gave Sylvie a sign. She sat down again. Jaja sighed:

'He'll lose again . . . He's not a bad boy . . .'

'I have to get dressed!' said Sylvie as she stood up and noticed that most of her body was exposed by her gaping dressing gown, quite innocently, as if it were the most natural thing in the world.

She went upstairs to the mezzanine, where she could be heard coming and going. Maigret got the impression that Jaja was listening to her.

'She sometimes bets on the horses too . . . She's the one who has lost the most with William's death . . .'

Maigret stood up suddenly, went into the bar and opened the outside door. But he was too late. Joseph was walking away briskly, without turning round. Just then a window opened.

'What's got into you?'

'Nothing . . . Just a thought . . .'

'Another drink? . . . You know, if you like the mutton . . .'

Sylvie was coming back down already; she was transformed, now unrecognizable in a navy-blue tailored suit which made her look younger. Under her white silk blouse her small trembling breasts were quite alluring, even though Maigret had already seen a fair bit of them. The skirt was tight over her narrow waist and taut buttocks. A pair of silk stockings had been pulled neatly up her legs.

'See you this evening?'

She too kissed Jaja on the forehead, then turned to

Maigret and hesitated. Did she want to leave without saying goodbye to him or did she want to hurl an insult? Either way, her look remained hostile. There was no danger of misreading her attitude.

'Good day . . . I presume you have no further need of me?'

She held herself quite tense. She waited a moment then set off with a determined step.

Jaja laughed as she refilled the glasses.

'Pay no attention . . . These girls don't have much sense. Would you like a plate so you can try some of my salad?'

The empty bar with its solitary front window looking out on to the street; upstairs, above the spiral staircase, the mezzanine, no doubt in a mess; the basement window and the courtyard, where the sun was slowly passing over.

A strange world, at the centre of which Maigret found himself settled in front of the remains of a fragrant salad in the company of a large woman who seemed to be propped up on her ample bosom and who sighed:

'When I was her age, we did things differently.'

She didn't need to explain further. He could imagine it quite well, somewhere in the vicinity of Porte Saint-Denis or Montmartre, in a gaudy silk dress, supervised through the windows of some bar by a constant companion.

'These days . . .'

She had had a glass or two too many. Her eyes welled up as she looked at Maigret. Her childlike mouth formed a pout that seemed to indicate impending tears.

'You remind me of William . . . That's where he sat . . . He too put his pipe down next to his plate when he ate . . . He had your shoulders . . . Do you know you look like him?'

She managed to wipe her eyes without crying.

4. *The Gentian*

It was that ambiguous rose-tinted hour when the sultriness of the setting sun dissipates in the coolness of the approaching night. Maigret left the Liberty Bar like someone leaving a house of ill-repute: hands deep in pockets, hat pulled down over the eyes.

Nevertheless, after a dozen or so steps, he felt the need to turn round, as if to make sure that the atmosphere he had left behind was real.

The bar was real enough, squeezed in between two houses, with its narrow street-front, painted a hideous brown, and the letters of its sign in yellow.

Inside the window there was a vase of flowers and, next to it, a sleeping cat.

Jaja must be sleeping somewhere too, in the back room, alone with the alarm clock, which was counting the minutes . . .

At the end of the narrow street normal life resumed: shops, people dressed in everyday clothes, cars, a tram, a policeman . . .

Then, to the right, the Croisette, which at this time of day looked like one of those watercolour adverts that the Cannes tourist office puts out in luxury magazines.

It was a mild, pleasant evening . . . People walking, in no hurry . . . Cars gliding by without a sound, as if they didn't have an engine . . . And all those light yachts in the harbour . . .

Maigret felt tired and sluggish, and yet he had no desire to return to Antibes. He walked around aimlessly, stopping for no particular reason, heading off again in no particular direction, as if he had left the conscious part of himself behind in Jaja's lair, next to the cluttered table where, at lunchtime, a prim Swedish steward had sat facing Sylvie and her bare breasts.

For ten years William Brown had spent several days a month there, in a state of warm lassitude, next to Jaja, who would start whining after a few drinks and would then go to sleep on her chair.

'The gentian, of course!'

Maigret was delighted to have found what he had been looking for for the last half-hour without even realizing it! Since he had left the Liberty Bar he had been struggling to pin it down, to strip away the surface image to get to its essence. And he had found it! He remembered what a friend had said when he had offered him an aperitif:

'What will you have?'

'A gentian.'

'Is that a fashionable new drink?'

'It's not a fashion! It's the drunk's last resort, my friend! You know the gentian. It's bitter. It's not even that alcoholic. When you've drunk every strong drink under the sun for the past thirty years, it's the only vice left: only that bitter kick has what it takes to stimulate the taste buds . . .'

That was it! A place without vice, without wickedness!

A bar where you went straight into the kitchen to be greeted like an old friend by Jaja!

And you drank while she prepared the food. You went to the neighbouring butcher yourself to find a nice joint. Sylvie would come down, eyes full of sleep, half naked, and you'd kiss her on the forehead, without even looking at her meagre breasts.

It wasn't very clean or very light. Nobody talked much. Conversation meandered somewhat, without conviction, like the people . . .

No more outside world, no bustle. Just a small rectangle of sunlight . . .

Eating, drinking . . . Snoozing, then drinking some more while Sylvie got dressed, pulling her stockings over her legs before setting off to work . . .

'See you later, Godfather!'

Wasn't it exactly the same as his friend's gentian? Wasn't the Liberty Bar the last port of call, when you had seen everything, tried everything by way of vices?

Women without beauty, without charms, without desire, whom you don't desire and kiss on the forehead while giving them a hundred francs to go and buy some stockings and then ask on their return:

'How was work?'

Maigret felt a bit oppressed by it all. He wanted to think about something else. He had stopped before the harbour, where a light mist was starting to spread out a few centimetres above the surface of the water.

He had gone past the small boats and the racing yachts. Ten metres away, a sailor was lowering a red flag with a crescent insignia on a huge white steamship that must have belonged to some pasha or other.

Somewhat nearer, he read the name of a forty-metre yacht picked out in gold lettering: *Ardena*.

No sooner did he bring to mind the face of the Swede he had met at Jaja's than he looked up and spotted him on the bridge, in white gloves, placing a tea tray on a rattan table.

The owner was leaning on a handrail and chatting to two young women. When he laughed he displayed an impressive set of teeth. A three-metre-long gangplank separated the group from Maigret; the inspector shrugged his shoulders and began to climb it, and almost burst out laughing when he saw the steward's face fall.

There are moments like this when you take a particular step, not because it is useful as such, but just in order to do something or to avoid thinking.

'Excuse me, sir . . .'

The owner had stopped laughing. He stood waiting, his face turned towards Maigret, as did the two women.

'A simple question, if you'd be so kind. Did you know a Monsieur Brown?'

'Does he own a boat?'

'He did once . . . William Brown . . .'

Maigret was barely waiting for a reply.

He looked at the man he had addressed, who must have been around forty-five and appeared very distinguished, standing between two women, half naked in their dresses.

He said to himself:

'Brown was like him! He too surrounded himself with beautiful, elegantly dressed women who had groomed themselves to perfection for the purpose of sexual allure! For his own amusement he took them to bars and bought champagne for everyone . . .'

The man replied, in a thick accent:

'If it's the Brown I'm thinking of, he used to own that large boat at the end . . . The *Pacific* . . . But it's been bought and sold at least a couple of times since then.'

'Thank you.'

The man and his two companions didn't really understand the purpose of Maigret's visit. They watched him walk away, and the inspector heard one of the women giggling.

The *Pacific* . . . There were only two boats of that size in the harbour, one of which was the one with the Turkish flag.

Only, the *Pacific* had an air of neglect about it. In several places the metal of the hull was visible where the paintwork had flaked off. The copper fittings were rusted with verdigris.

A scrawled notice on the bulwarks: 'For Sale'.

It was that time of day when the yacht sailors, all scrubbed up and in smart uniforms, were heading off into town in groups, like soldiers.

When Maigret walked back past the *Ardena*, he could feel the three pairs of eyes on him and he suspected that the steward was scrutinizing him from some nook or cranny in the bridge.

The streets were lit up. Maigret had a bit of difficulty finding the garage again, where he had one last matter to clear up.

'What time did Brown come by on Friday to collect his car?'

They had to ask the mechanic.

A few minutes before five! In other words, he had just enough time to drive straight back to Cap d'Antibes.

'Was he alone? Was there anyone waiting for him outside? And are you sure he wasn't wounded?'

William Brown had left the Liberty Bar around two o'clock. What did he do in those three hours?

There was no need for Maigret to stay in Cannes any longer. He waited for the bus, settled himself in a corner and let his gaze drift over the procession of car headlights streaming along the main road.

The first person he saw as he got off the bus at Place Macé was Inspector Boutigues, who was sitting on the terrace of the Café Glacier and who jumped to his feet.

'We've been looking for you since morning! . . . Take a seat . . . What will you have? . . . Waiter! Two Pernods!'

'Not for me! . . . A gentian!' said Maigret, who wanted to find out for himself what that beverage tasted like.

'I asked the taxi-drivers first of all. Since none of them had picked you up, I checked out the bus drivers. That's how I know you went to Cannes . . .'

He was talking quickly, heatedly.

In spite of himself, Maigret looked at him with round eyes. But that didn't stop the little inspector from ploughing on:

'There are only five or six restaurants where you can get a decent meal . . . I phoned each of them . . . Where on earth did you have lunch?'

Boutigues would have been very surprised if Maigret had told him the truth, if he had told him about the mutton and the garlic salad in Jaja's kitchen, and the small glasses, and Sylvie . . .

'The examining magistrate doesn't want to do anything without consulting you . . . Plus, there's news – the son has arrived . . .'

'Whose son?'

And Maigret gave a grimace, because he had just drunk a mouthful of gentian.

'Brown's son . . . He was in Amsterdam when . . .'

'Brown has a son?'

'More than one . . . By his real wife, who lives in Australia . . . One of them is in Europe, taking care of the wool . . .'

'The wool?'

Right at this moment, Boutigues must have had a dim opinion of Maigret. But the latter was still in the Liberty Bar! More precisely, he was remembering the waiter who bet on the horses and to whom Sylvie had spoken through the window . . .

'Yes, the Browns have one of the biggest businesses in Australia. They raise sheep and export the wool to Europe. One of the sons oversees the ranches; another, based in Sydney, takes care of the exports; the third, in Europe, travels from port to port, depending on whether the wool is destined for Liverpool, Le Havre or Hamburg. He's the one who . . .'

'And what did he have to say?'

'That his father should be buried as soon as possible and that he would pay . . . He has a very busy schedule . . . He has to catch a plane tomorrow evening . . .'

'Is he in Antibes?'

'Actually, in Juan-les-Pins . . . He wanted a luxury hotel, with a suite solely for his use . . . It seems he needed a telephone link throughout the night to Nice, so that he could call Antwerp, Amsterdam or who knows where else.'

'Has he visited the villa?'

'I suggested that to him. He refused.'

'So what has he done, then?'

'He has seen the magistrate. That's all. He insisted that everything should expedited. And he asked how much.'

'How much what?'

'How much it would cost.'

Maigret scanned Place Macé with an absent air. Boutigues went on:

'The magistrate has been waiting for you at his office the whole afternoon. He can hardly refuse the request for a burial now that the post mortem has been completed . . . Brown's son phoned three times and in the end he was told that the funeral could go ahead first thing tomorrow morning . . .'

'First thing?'

'Yes, to avoid the crowds . . . That's why I was looking for you . . . They are going to close the coffin tonight. So if you want to see Brown before they . . .'

'No.'

No, Maigret really didn't want to see the body. He felt he knew William Brown well enough without it!

The terrace was full of people. Boutigues noticed that several tables were observing them, a fact that didn't exactly displease him. Nevertheless he murmured:

'Let's keep our voices down . . .'

'Where will they bury him?'

'At Antibes cemetery . . . The hearse will be at the mortuary at seven o'clock in the morning . . . I just have to confirm it officially with Brown's son.'

'And the two women?'

'We haven't decided . . . It's possible the son might prefer . . . ?'

'What hotel did you say he was in?'

'The Provençal. Do you want to see him?'

'Until tomorrow!' said Maigret. 'I suppose you will be at the funeral?'

He was in a strange mood, at once joyful and macabre! He got a taxi to the Provençal, where he was met by a doorman, then another employee in a braided uniform, then finally by a thin young man in black, lurking behind a desk.

'Monsieur Brown? I will see if he is available . . . Would you care to tell me your name?'

Bells ringing, the porter coming and going. Maigret had to wait at least five minutes before someone came to fetch him and led him down interminable corridors until they reached a door marked 37. From behind the door came the sound of a typewriter, and an irritable voice:

'Come in!'

Maigret found himself face to face with Brown Junior, the one in charge of the European branch of the wool firm.

Ageless. Maybe thirty, but then again, maybe forty. A tall, thin man, with chiselled features, close-cropped hair, dressed in a smart suit, a pearl tiepin in his black tie with a white stripe.

Not a hint of disorder or unpredictability. Not a hair out of place. And not the slightest reaction at the sight of his visitor.

'Could you bear with me for a moment? Please take a seat.'

There was a typist sitting at the Louis XV table. A secretary was talking in English on the telephone.

And Brown was just finishing dictating a cable, in English, which was to do with damages because of a dockers' strike.

The secretary called out: 'Mister Brown,' and handed him the phone.

'Hello! . . . Hello! . . . Yes!'

He listened for a while, without a word of interruption, then hung up, saying as he did so:

'No!'

He pressed an electric bell button and asked Maigret:

'A port?'

'No, thank you.'

But as the maître d'hôtel turned up, he ordered anyway:

'One port!'

He did this in a totally calm way, with evident concern, as if the destiny of the world hung on even the smallest of his actions, gestures or facial expressions.

'Take your typing to the bedroom,' he said to the typist, indicating the adjoining room.

And to his secretary:

'Get me the examining magistrate.'

Finally he sat down, crossing his legs with a sigh:

'I'm tired. Are you in charge of the investigation?'

And he slid the port that the servant had brought over to Maigret.

'Such a ridiculous tale, isn't it?'

'Not ridiculous at all,' Maigret muttered in his least agreeable voice.

'I meant to say awkward . . .'

'Of course! It's always awkward when you're stabbed to death in the back . . .'

The young man stood up impatiently, opened the door to the bedroom, made as if to give some orders in English, returned to Maigret and offered him a cigarette case.

'No, thank you. I'm a pipe man.'

The man picked up a tin of English tobacco from a pedestal table.

'I smoke shag!' said Maigret, taking a packet from his pocket.

Brown prowled around the room with long strides.

'I take it you know that my father led a very . . . scandalous life . . .'

'He had a mistress!'

'And more besides! Much more! You need to know this, otherwise you run the risk of making . . . how do you say . . . a gaffe . . .'

He was interrupted by the telephone. The secretary ran over and replied this time in German while Brown shook his head at him. And since the secretary was having trouble getting off the phone, the young man went and took the receiver from his hands and hung up.

'My father came to France a long time ago, without my mother . . . And he almost ruined us . . .'

Brown didn't stay put. As he was talking, he had closed the door of the bedroom on his secretary. He tapped the glass of port with his finger.

'You're not drinking?'

'No, thank you.'

He shrugged his shoulders impatiently.

'We appointed a legal guardian . . . My mother was very unhappy . . . She worked so hard . . .'

'Ah! It was your mother who looked after things?'

'With my uncle, yes.'

'Your mother's brother, I'm assuming.'

'Yes! My father had lost all . . . dignity . . . yes, dignity . . . so the least said the better . . . Do you understand?'

Maigret had never taken his eyes off him, and that seemed to upset the young man. Especially as this heavy gaze was impossible to decipher. Perhaps it was meant to convey nothing. On the other hand, perhaps it was terribly threatening.

'One question, Monsieur Brown – Monsieur Harry Brown, as I see from your luggage labels. Where were you last Wednesday?'

Brown walked the length of the room twice before he replied:

'What are you implying?'

'I'm not implying anything. I'm simply asking you where you were.'

'Is it important?'

'Maybe it is, maybe it isn't.'

'I was in Marseille, because of the arrival of the *Glasco*! A ship carrying wool from home which is now in Amsterdam unable to unload because of the dockers' strike.'

'You didn't see your father?'

'I didn't . . .'

'Another question, the last. Who paid your father's allowance? And how much was it?'

'Me! Five thousand francs a month . . . Do you want to reveal that to the papers?'

The sound of the typewriter could still be heard: the bell at the end of each line, the shunt of the carriage return.

Maigret stood up and picked up his hat.

'Thank you.'

'That's it?'

'That's it . . . Thank you.'

The telephone rang again, but the young man showed no sign of answering it. He merely watched, as if incredulous, as Maigret made for the door.

Then, in desperation, he grabbed an envelope from the table.

'I have something here for the police welfare fund . . .'

Maigret was already in the corridor. A little later, he was descending the sumptuous staircase, crossing the lobby, preceded by a liveried flunkey.

At nine o'clock he dined alone in the dining room of the Hôtel Bacon while flicking through the telephone directory. He asked for three Cannes numbers in quick succession. Only the third one got a reply:

'Yes, it's next to . . .'

'Excellent! Would you be so kind as to tell Madame Jaja

that the funeral will take place tomorrow at seven o'clock in Antibes? . . . Yes, the funeral . . . She will understand . . .'

He took a short walk around the room. From the window he could see, five hundred metres away, Brown's white villa, where two windows were lit up.

Did he have the energy?

No! He needed sleep.

'They are on the phone, aren't they?'

'Yes, inspector. Do you want me to call them?'

A sweet little maid in a white bonnet, who was scurrying round the room like a mouse.

'Sir, I have one of the ladies on the line . . .'

Maigret took the receiver.

'Hello! . . . It's the inspector here . . . Yes . . . I wasn't able to come and see you . . . The funeral is at seven tomorrow morning . . . What's that? . . . No! Not this evening . . . I have work to do . . . Goodnight, madame . . .'

It must have been the mother. No doubt she was running madly to announce the news to her daughter. Then they would both be discussing what they had to do.

The landlady of the Hôtel Bacon came into the room, smiling blandly.

'Did you enjoy the bouillabaisse? I made it especially for you, since you . . .'

The bouillabaisse? Maigret searched his memory.

'Ah yes! Excellent! Very fine!' he forced himself to say with a polite smile.

But he couldn't remember it. It was lost in the fog of useless things, stashed higgledy-piggledy alongside Boutigues, the bus, the garage . . .

Of all the culinary details, only one stood out: the leg of mutton at Jaja's, and the salad with the fragrance of garlic . . .

No, wait! There was another one: the sweet smell of the port that he didn't drink at the Provençal, which mingled with the sickly scent of Brown's after-shave.

'Bring me up a bottle of Vittel!' he said as he mounted the stairs.

5. The Funeral of William Brown

The sun was already intoxicating, and although all the shutters were closed and the pavements deserted in the town's streets, the market was starting to come to life. It was the light and carefree sort of life of people who get up early and have time to fill and spend it whining in French and Italian rather than bustling about.

The yellow façade of the town hall with its double front steps stood right in the middle of the market. The mortuary was in the basement.

It was there, at ten minutes to seven, that a hearse drew up, completely black and incongruous in the middle of the flowers and vegetables. Maigret arrived at almost the same time and saw Boutigues arriving in haste, with his waistcoat unbuttoned, having only got out of bed ten minutes earlier.

'We've got time for a quick drink . . . There's no one here yet . . .'

And he went into a small bar and ordered a rum.

'It's been really complicated, you know. The son forgot to tell us how much he wanted to spend on the coffin. I phoned him yesterday evening. He said he didn't care about the price as long as it was of good quality. But there wasn't a solid-oak coffin in the whole of Antibes. We had to bring one in from Cannes at eleven o'clock last night . . . Then there was the ceremony to think about . . . Should it be a church ceremony or not? . . . I phoned the Provençal and they told me Brown had already gone to bed . . . I did my best . . . As you can see . . .'

He pointed to a church a hundred metres away across the market square, whose door was draped in black.

Maigret didn't want to say anything, but he had got the impression that Brown Junior was a Protestant rather than a Catholic.

The bar was on the corner of a small street and had a door on each side. Just as Maigret and Boutigues were leaving by one door, a man entered by the other, and the inspector caught his eye.

It was Joseph, the waiter from Cannes, who was in two minds whether to wave or not and in the end settled on a half-hearted gesture. Maigret assumed that Joseph had brought Jaja and Sylvie from Cannes. He was right. They were walking in front of him, heading towards the hearse. Jaja was out of breath already. And Sylvie, who seemed anxious not to arrive late, was tugging her along.

Sylvie was wearing her little blue suit that made her look like a smart young woman. As for Jaja, she was unused to walking. Maybe her feet were hurting, or her legs were swollen. She was dressed in very shiny black silk. They must have both had to get up around five in the morning to catch the first bus. An unprecedented event, no doubt, at the Liberty Bar!

Boutigues asked him:

'Who are they?'

'I don't know . . .' Maigret replied vaguely.

But at that moment the two women stopped and turned round, as they had reached the hearse. And when Jaja spotted Maigret, she dashed over to him.

'We're not late, are we? . . . Where is he?'

Sylvie had rings round her eyes and was still giving Maigret an unfriendly look.

'Did Joseph come with you?'

She was about to lie.

'Who told you that?'

Boutigues was standing some distance away. Maigret spotted a taxi which, unable to cross the square because of the crowded market, had stopped at the corner of a street.

The two women who got out were an amazing sight, for they were in full mourning regalia, with crepe veils almost brushing the ground.

It was so unexpected, in the sunshine, amid the buzz of joyous life! Maigret murmured to Jaja:

'Allow me . . .'

Boutigues was troubled. He asked the head pall-bearer, who wanted to go to fetch the coffin, to wait a moment.

'We're not too late, are we?' the old woman asked. 'Our taxi failed to turn up . . .'

And then immediately her gaze fell on Jaja and Sylvie.

'Who are they?'

'I don't know.'

'I assume they won't interfere . . .'

Another taxi pulled up, its door opening before it had

come to a complete stop, and from it Harry Brown emerged, impeccably dressed in black, his blond hair well groomed, his complexion fresh. His secretary, also in black, accompanied him, carrying a wreath of natural flowers.

At the same moment, Maigret noticed that Sylvie had disappeared. He spotted her in the middle of the market, next to a flowerseller, and when she returned she was carrying an enormous bouquet of Nice violets.

Did this inspire the two Martini women with the same idea? They were clearly having a discussion as they approached the flowerseller. The old woman counted out some coins, and the young woman chose mimosas.

Meanwhile, Brown had taken up a position a few metres from the hearse, limiting himself to a wave in the direction of Maigret and Boutigues.

'I'd better inform him of what I have arranged for the service . . .' the latter sighed.

The part of the market nearest to them slowed its pace, and people watched the unfolding spectacle. But a mere twenty metres away, it was business as normal: the din of shouts and laughter, all the flowers, fruits and vegetables under the sun, and the smell of garlic and mimosa.

There were four pallbearers carrying the coffin, which was enormous and weighed down by a profusion of bronze ornaments. Boutigues came back.

'He doesn't seem to care. He just shrugged his shoulders . . .'

The crowd parted. The horses started walking. Harry

Brown advanced stiffly, hat in hand, looking at the tips of his polished shoes.

The four women hesitated. They exchanged glances. Then, as the crowd closed in behind them, they found themselves unintentionally walking side by side, just behind Brown Junior and his secretary.

The doors of the church were wide open; the interior was completely empty and delightfully cool.

Brown stood at the top of the steps until they had removed the coffin from the hearse. He was used to ceremonial occasions. It didn't bother him one bit that he was the focus of everyone's attention.

More than that, he quietly studied the four women, without appearing overly curious.

The orders had come too late. They realized at the last minute that they had failed to inform the organist. The priest called Boutigues forwards and whispered to him; when the latter returned from the sacristy, he was quite upset and announced to Maigret:

'There won't be any music . . . We'd have to wait at least another quarter of an hour . . . At least! The organist must be out fishing for mackerel . . .'

A few people wandered into the church, glanced around and then left. And Brown continued to stand to attention and look around him with the same light curiosity.

It was a swift service, without an organ, without a eulogy. A sprinkling of holy water from the aspergillum. And then straight afterwards the pallbearers carried the coffin out.

It was already hot outside. They passed in front of a hairdresser's window as a barber in a white jacket was opening the shutters. A man was shaving before his open window. And the people on their way to work turned round astonished at the sight of this tiny cortège, where the derisory escort was so out of kilter with the pomp of the funeral carriage.

The two women from Cannes and the two women from Antibes were still walking in a row, though they kept a metre apart. They were followed by an empty taxi. Boutigues, who had taken on the responsibility for this ceremony, was nervous.

'Do you think there will be a scandal?'

There wasn't. The cemetery, with all its flowers, was as colourful as the market. At the open grave they found the priest and an altar boy, whom they hadn't noticed arrive.

Harry Brown was invited to cast the first handful of earth. Then there was a moment of uncertainty. The old woman in mourning dress pushed her daughter forwards and followed her.

Brown had already gone striding off to the empty taxi that was waiting at the cemetery gate.

Another moment of uncertainty. Maigret stood back, with Boutigues. Jaja and Sylvie didn't dare leave without saying goodbye to him. Only the women in mourning got there before them.

'That was his son, wasn't it? . . . I suppose he'll want to come to the villa?'

'Perhaps. I don't know . . .'

But they had eyes only for Jaja and Sylvie. They alone grabbed their attention.

'Where are they from? . . . People like that shouldn't be allowed . . .'

There were birds singing in all the trees. The grave-diggers shovelled the earth into the grave in a regular rhythm, and, as it filled up, the sound became more muffled. They had placed the wreath and the two bouquets on the neighbouring grave while they worked. And Sylvie stood turned towards them, staring fixedly, her lips pale.

Jaja was getting impatient. She was waiting for the other two to leave so that she could talk to Maigret. She wiped her brow, because it was hot. She must have been having difficulty standing.

'Yes . . . I'll be seeing you soon . . .'

The black veils headed for the exit. Jaja approached with a huge sigh of relief.

'Is that them? . . . Was he really married?'

Sylvie held back, still watching the grave, which was now nearly filled in.

And Boutigues was the same bag of nerves. He didn't dare come to listen to the conversation.

'Was it the son who paid for the coffin?'

It was obvious that Jaja was ill at ease.

'What a strange funeral!' she said. 'I don't know why, but I'd never imagined it like that . . . I wouldn't even have been able to cry . . .'

Now the emotion hit her. She looked at the cemetery and succumbed to some undefined malaise.

'It wasn't even a sad occasion! . . . You'd have thought it was . . .'

'You'd have thought it was what?'

'I don't know . . . It was as if it wasn't a real funeral.'

She stifled a sob, dried her eyes and turned towards Sylvie.

'Come . . . Joseph is waiting for us . . .'

The cemetery caretaker was sitting in his doorway, slicing an eel.

'What do you think?'

Boutigues was concerned. He too had the vague feeling that something wasn't quite right. Maigret lit his pipe.

'I think William Brown was murdered!' he replied.

'Obviously!'

They were wandering round the streets, where the shops had already drawn canopies over their windows. The barber from that morning was sitting outside his door, reading his newspaper. In Place Macé they spotted the two women from Cannes and Joseph, waiting for the bus.

'Fancy a quick one?' suggested Boutigues, indicating the café terrace.

Maigret accepted. He was filled by an almost overwhelming laziness. A succession of images flashed across his retinas, all confused, and he made no attempt to sort them into any order.

On the terrace of the Glacier, for example, he half closed his eyes. The sun was baking his eyelids. His intertwined eyelashes formed a grill of shadow, behind which people and objects took on an almost fairy-tale appearance.

He saw Joseph helping Jaja to haul herself up on to the bus. Then a small man dressed all in white, with a colonial helmet on his head, walked by slowly, leading a chow chow with a purple tongue.

Other images became mixed up with the real ones: William Brown, at the wheel of his old car, driving his women from shop to shop, sometimes with only his pyjamas on under his overcoat and with stubble on his chin.

By this time the son would be back at the Provençal, in his luxury suite, dictating cables, answering the telephone, pacing up and down with his regular stride.

'It's an odd business!' sighed Boutigues, who had to fill every silence, as he crossed and uncrossed his legs first one way, then the other. 'What a shame they forgot to inform the organist!'

'Yes! William Brown was murdered . . .'

It was for his own sake that Maigret repeated this, to convince himself that, in spite of everything, a drama really had occurred.

His detachable collar felt tight. His forehead was damp. He looked with relish at the large cube of ice floating in his drink.

'Brown was murdered . . . He left the villa, as he did every month, to go to Cannes. He left his car at the garage. He visited a bank or some business to collect the monthly allowance that his son provided for him. Then he spent a few days at the Liberty Bar.'

A few days of warm laziness like the one that had overcome Maigret.

A few days in slippers, slouching from one chair to another, eating and drinking with Jaja, watching a semi-naked Sylvie come and go . . .

'On Friday, at two o'clock, he left . . . At five o'clock, he picked up his car and, a quarter of an hour later, he collapsed, fatally wounded, on the steps of his villa, while his women, thinking he was drunk, swore at him from the window . . . He had about two thousand francs on him, as usual . . .'

Maigret didn't say any of this out loud, he merely thought it as he watched the passers-by filing in front of the grill of his eyelashes.

It was Boutigues who broke the silence:

'Who would have an interest in seeing him dead?'

There it was: the dangerous question. His two women? Didn't they, on the contrary, have an interest in keeping him alive as long as possible since, out of the two thousand francs that he brought home each month, they managed to save a small amount?

The women from Cannes? They will have lost one of their few customers, someone who kept the whole household fed for a week and paid for stockings for one of them and paid the gas and electricity bills of the other . . .

No! In terms of material advantage, only Harry Brown stood to gain anything, as he no longer had to pay out five thousand francs a month.

But what is five thousand francs to a family that sells wool by the shipload?

Boutigues sighed again:

'I'm beginning to think the people round here are right, and it's a spying matter . . .'

'Waiter! Same again!' said Maigret.

He regretted it immediately. He wanted to cancel the order, but didn't dare.

He didn't dare out of fear of admitting to his weakness. He would remember this later, remember sitting on the terrace of the Café Glacier, remember Place Macé . . .

It was one of his rare moments of weakness! Total weakness! The air was warm. A little girl was selling mimosas at the corner of the street in her bare feet, her legs tanned.

A fat grey torpedo with nickel accessories slid past silently, carrying three women in summer pyjamas and a young man with a thin, matinee-idol moustache on their way to the beach.

It smelled of holidays. The previous evening Cannes harbour, with the setting sun, had also had that smell of holidays, especially the *Ardena*, whose owner swaggered in front of two girls with gorgeous figures.

Maigret was dressed in black, as was his wont in Paris. He had his bowler hat with him, which didn't belong here.

A notice in blue letters right in front of him announced:

Casino of Juan-les-Pins
Golden Rain Grand Gala

And the ice cube melted slowly in the opal-coloured glass.

Holidays! Watching the silken seabed, leaning over

the side of a boat painted green or orange . . . Having a nap under a stone pine, listening to the buzzing of large flies . . .

Above all, not worrying about some man whom he didn't know who happened to get stabbed in the back!

Or about those women whom Maigret didn't even know before yesterday evening and whose faces haunted him, as if he had been the one who slept with them!

A terrible job! The air smelled of melting bitumen, Boutigues had pinned a fresh red carnation to the lapel of his light-grey jacket.

William Brown? . . . He was buried . . . What else did he want? . . . Was it anything to do with Maigret? . . . Was it he who once owned one of the biggest yachts in Europe? . . . Was it he who had shacked up with the two Martini women, the mother with the plastered face and the daughter with the callipygian figure? . . . Was it he who had immersed himself blissfully in the crapulous laziness of the Liberty Bar? . . . There were small warm puffs of wind that stroked your cheeks . . . The people walking past were on holiday . . . Everyone was on holiday here! . . . Life was one long holiday!

Even Boutigues, who was unable to be silent and who muttered:

'Deep down, I'm happy that they didn't want me to take responsibility for . . .'

Now Maigret stopped peering at the world through his lashes. He turned to his companion, his face somewhat flushed by the heat and by somnolence. His pupils seemed a little confused, but after a few seconds took on their usual sharpness.

'That's right!' he said as he stood up. 'Waiter! How much is that?'

'Allow me.'

'No, I insist.'

He tossed a few notes on to the table.

Yes, it was an hour he would remember well, because he was tempted simply not to bother, to let everything go, like everyone else, to take things as they came.

And the weather was glorious!

'Are you off? . . . Have you got something in mind?'

No! His head was too full of sun, of languor. He didn't have the slightest thing in mind. And, as he didn't want to lie, he murmured:

'William Brown was murdered!'

And he thought to himself:

'And none of them could give a damn!'

None of these people basking in the sun like lizards, who would be spending the evening at the Golden Rain Gala.

'I'm off to work!' he said.

He shook Boutigues' hand. He walked off. He stopped as a 300,000-franc car drove past with a slip of an eighteen-year-old girl at the wheel; she looked straight ahead and frowned.

'Brown was murdered . . .' he continued to repeat.

He was learning not to underestimate the South. He turned his back on the Café Glacier. And, in order not to lapse into temptation again, he started to dictate to himself, as if to a subordinate:

'Find out what Brown was doing on Friday afternoon between two and five.'

So he would have to go to Cannes! On the bus!

And he stood waiting, his hands in his pockets, pipe between his teeth, a grumpy look on his face, beneath a streetlamp.

6. The Shameful Companion

For the next few hours, Maigret devoted himself to some dreary legwork of the sort he normally delegated to junior officers. But he felt the need to move, to give himself the illusion of decisive action.

In Vice they knew about Sylvie – she was on their books.

'I've never had any problems with her,' said the sergeant who was in charge of her neighbourhood. 'She's a quiet one. Has a check-up pretty regularly . . .'

'And the Liberty Bar?'

'You've heard about it? A strange joint. It's intrigued us for a while, and indeed intrigues a lot of other people. Almost every month we get an anonymous tip-off about it. At first we suspected Big Jaja of selling narcotics. We put her under surveillance, and I can vouch for the fact it isn't true . . . Others made out that the back room was used as a meeting place for people with certain proclivities . . .'

'I know that's not true!' said Maigret.

'Yes . . . The truth is even odder . . . Jaja attracts these old types who don't want anything out of life except to get drunk in her company. Besides, she has a small pension, as her husband died in an accident . . .'

'I know!'

In another department, Maigret got some information on Joseph.

'We're keeping an eye on him, because he's a regular at the racetrack, but we've never made anything stick.'

Maigret was drawing a blank right across the board. He started to walk around town with his hands in his pockets and that stubborn look that usually expressed that he was in a bad mood.

He began by visiting the luxury hotels, where he checked the registers. In between, he had lunch at a restaurant next to the station, and by three in the afternoon he knew that Harry Brown had not slept in Cannes on either the Tuesday or the Wednesday night.

It was pathetic. Doing something for the sake of doing something!

'Brown Junior might have come from Marseille by car and might have left the same day . . .'

Maigret went back to Vice, where he picked up the photo of Sylvie they had on file. He already had the picture of William Brown in his pocket, which he had taken from the villa.

And he entered a new milieu: the small hotels, especially those around the harbour, which rented out rooms not just by the night but also by the hour.

The landlords realized straight away that he was from the police. They were the sort of people who feared that more than anything.

'Wait here. I'll ask the chambermaid . . .'

And the inspector discovered a whole decadent underworld in those dark corridors.

'The big fellow? . . . No, I don't recall seeing him here . . .'

Maigret showed William Brown's photo first, followed by that of Sylvie.

Almost everyone knew her.

'She came here . . . But it was a long time ago . . .'

'At night?'

'Oh no! When she came with someone it was always a "short stay" . . .'

Hôtel Bellevue . . . Hôtel du Port . . . Hôtel Bristol . . . Hôtel d'Auvergne . . .

Then there were others, mostly in the sidestreets, mostly very discreet, showing no sign of their existence to passers-by other than marbled nameplates alongside open corridors saying: 'Running water. Reasonable prices'.

Sometimes Maigret went more upmarket, found a carpet on the stairs . . . Other times he came across a furtive couple in the corridor who turned their heads away . . .

And on the way out he would see the harbour, where a number of international-class six-metre racing yachts were drawn up on the beach.

Some sailors were painting them carefully, watched by groups of curious onlookers.

'No dramas,' they had said in Paris.

Well, if it went on like this, they would be satisfied. There would be no drama at all for the simple reason that Maigret would find nothing!

He smoked pipe after pipe, filling one before the other was even extinguished, for he always carried two or three in his pockets.

And he took a real dislike to the place, because a woman was bothering him to buy some shellfish and a small boy ran up to him, barefoot, and jumped in front of his feet, then burst out laughing as he looked at him.

'Do you know this man?'

He was showing William Brown's photo for the twentieth time.

'He never came here.'

'Or this woman?'

'Sylvie? . . . She's upstairs . . .'

'Alone?'

The landlord shrugged his shoulders, called upstairs:

'Albert! . . . Come downstairs a moment . . .'

A scruffy valet, who looked right through the inspector.

'Is Sylvie still up there?'

'Number 7 . . .'

'Have they ordered any drinks?'

'No.'

'In that case, they won't be long!' said the landlord. 'If you want to talk to her, you just need to wait . . .'

The place was called the Hôtel Beauséjour, and it was on a street running parallel to the harbour, directly opposite a bakery.

Did Maigret want to see Sylvie again? Did he have one or two questions to ask her?

He didn't even know himself. He was tired. There was something threatening about his demeanour, as if he had almost had enough.

He wasn't going to wait outside the hotel, for the baker's wife opposite was watching him through her window with a knowing look.

Did Sylvie have so many lovers that occasionally one of

them would be waiting his turn downstairs? That was it! Maigret was furious that he should be taken for one of the girl's clients.

He walked to the corner of the street with the idea of touring the block to kill time. As he arrived on the quay-side, he turned round to look at a taxi parked along the pavement whose driver was pacing up and down.

He couldn't put his finger on what had caught his attention. He did a double take. It wasn't so much the taxi as the man who reminded him of something, and suddenly his image connected to the memory of that morning's funeral.

'You're from Antibes, aren't you?'

'Juan-les-Pins!'

'You followed a funeral procession to the cemetery this morning . . .'

'That's right! Why the interest?'

'Is it the same customer you've brought here?' The taxi-driver looked at him from head to toe, unsure whether or not he should reply.

'Why are you asking me this?'

'Police . . . Well, then?'

'Yes, same one . . . He booked me yesterday midday, on a day rate.'

'Where is he right now?'

'I don't know . . . He went off that way . . .'

The man pointed to a street, then suddenly asked anxiously:

'Hey, you're not going to arrest him before he pays me, are you?'

Maigret forgot to smoke. He stood there a moment quite still, staring at the taxi's old-fashioned bonnet, then suddenly, struck by the thought that the couple might have left the hotel already, he dashed back to the Beauséjour.

The baker's wife saw him arrive and called her husband, who emerged from the back of the shop and came to the window, his face white with flour.

Too bad! Now Maigret was having a laugh at their expense.

'Room 7.'

He looked up at the façade, trying to work out which of the windows with drawn curtains corresponded to room number 7. He didn't dare celebrate yet.

And yet . . . No! This wasn't a coincidence . . . On the contrary, it was the first time that he had found a link between two elements of this case . . .

Sylvie and Harry Brown together in a rented room near the harbour!

Twenty times he was able to cover the hundred metres to the corner of the quay. Twenty times he saw the taxi in the same spot. As for the driver, he had come to stand at the end of the street as if he wanted to keep an eye on his customer himself.

Finally, the glass door at the end of the corridor opened. Sylvie came out quickly on to the pavement and almost bumped into Maigret.

'Good day,' he said.

She froze. He had never seen her look so pale. And when she opened her mouth to speak, no sound came out.

'Is your companion getting dressed?'

Her head swung this way and that like a weathervane. She dropped her bag, which Maigret picked up. She literally snatched it back off him as if she were afraid of nothing more than to see him open it.

'One moment!'

'Excuse me . . . I'm expected somewhere . . . You can walk with me if you like . . .'

'I don't want to walk . . . Especially not that way . . .'

She was winsome rather than pretty, because of her large eyes, which darted over his whole face. It was obvious she was in a nervous state; her anxiety was making her breathless.

'What do you want from me?'

She seemed to be on the point of running away. To prevent her, Maigret took her hand and held it in his, a gesture that the bakers opposite might have interpreted as one of affection.

'Is Harry still here?'

'I don't understand . . .'

'Fine! We'll wait for him together . . . Be careful! . . . Don't do anything stupid . . . Let go of the bag . . .'

For Maigret had made another grab for it. Through the silky material he could feel what seemed to be a wad of banknotes.

'Don't make a scene! . . . There are people watching us . . .'

And passers-by too. They must have thought that Maigret and Sylvie were simply haggling over the price.

'I beg you . . .'

'No!'

Then, more quietly:

'If you don't calm down, I'll use the handcuffs!'

She looked at him, eyes still wide with fright, then, whether discouraged or subdued, she lowered her head.

Harry didn't seem to be in any hurry to come down . . .

She didn't say a word, didn't attempt to deny or explain.

'Did you know him before?'

They were standing in full sun. Sylvie's face was perspiring.

She seemed to be desperately looking for some inspiration that eluded her.

'Listen . . .'

'I'm listening!'

No, she changed her mind! She didn't say another word. She bit hard on her lip.

'Is Joseph waiting for you somewhere?'

'Joseph?'

She was panicking. Steps could be heard on the hotel staircase. Sylvie was trembling. She dared not look into the dark interior.

The steps approached, resounding on the floor tiles. The glass door opened and closed again, and then time seemed to stand still.

Harry Brown, barely distinguishable in the gloom, had spotted the couple.

It was a brief moment. He started walking again. He had a lot of nerve. He walked past, his body held straight, acknowledging Maigret with a brief nod.

Maigret was still holding Sylvie's limp hand. To catch up with the receding figure of Brown he would have to let her go.

What a farcical scene that would be for the audience in the bakery . . .

'Come with me,' he said to his companion.

'Are you arresting me?'

'Don't bother your head about that . . .'

He had to make a phone call urgently. He didn't want to leave Sylvie on her own at any price. There were some cafés nearby. He went into one and dragged the young woman into the cabin with him.

A few moments later he had Inspector Boutigues on the line.

'Run to the Hôtel Provençal. Ask Harry Brown, politely but firmly, not to leave Antibes until I get there. If necessary, prevent him from leaving . . .'

And Sylvie listened to this, slumping. Her spirit was broken, she didn't have the slightest inclination to rebel.

'What would you like to drink?' he asked her, when they got back to the table.

'I don't mind.'

He kept his eye on the handbag. The waiter observed them, aware that something unusual was going on. A young girl went from table to table offering bouquets of violets; Maigret took one, handed it to his companion, searched through his pockets with a distracted air and then, when she was least expecting it, grabbed the bag.

'Do you mind? . . . I have no change . . .'

He did it so quickly and in such a matter-of-fact way that she didn't have time to protest. Nothing more than a fleeting grasp of her fingers on the handle.

The young flowerseller waited patiently, choosing another bouquet from her basket. Maigret looked for some loose change beneath a fat wad of thousand-franc notes.

'Right, let's go,' he said, standing up.

He was agitated too. He was in a hurry to be somewhere else, to not have all these curious eyes directed at him.

'Shall we go and say hello to dear old Jaja?'

Sylvie followed him docilely. She was ground down. And there was nothing to distinguish them from any other couple who walked past, except for the fact that Maigret was holding his companion's handbag.

'You go first!'

She went down one step into the bar and made her way to the glass door at the back. Behind the net curtain could be seen a man's back; he jumped to his feet when the pair of them arrived.

It was Yan, the Swedish steward, who blushed to the roots of his hair when he recognized Maigret.

'You again? . . . Well, then, my friend, would you be so kind as to go for a walk . . . ?'

Jaja didn't understand. Sylvie's face told her that there was something unusual going on. So she would not be displeased to see the sailor make himself scarce.

'Are you coming tomorrow, Yan?'

'I don't know . . .'

Standing with his cap in hand, he wasn't sure how to get away, troubled as he was by the inspector's glowering look.

'Yes . . . It's OK . . . Bye . . .' the latter said impatiently, opening the door to usher him out.

He locked the door with a brusque turn of the key. He said to Sylvie:

'You can take your hat off.'

Jaja hazarded, in a timid voice:

'You bumped into each other . . .'

'Exactly. We bumped into each other.'

She didn't even dare offer him a drink, so aware was she of the heavy atmosphere in the room. To keep her composure, she picked a newspaper off the floor, folded it up and then went to check something on her stove.

Maigret filled a pipe, quite gently. He went to the stove himself and, rolling up a piece of newspaper, lit it in the grate.

Sylvie stayed standing next to the table. She had taken off her hat and placed it in front of her. Then Maigret sat down, opened the bag and began counting out the banknotes, which he lined up between the dirty glasses.

'Eighteen . . . Nineteen . . . Twenty . . . Twenty thousand francs!'

Jaja had turned round in one movement and was looking at the money with bewilderment. She was struggling to make sense of it.

'What is this . . .?'

'Oh, nothing, really!' Maigret growled. 'Sylvie found herself a lover more generous than most, that's all! And do you know his name? Harry Brown . . .'

He had made himself at home, his elbows resting on the table, his pipe in his mouth, his bowler hat pushed back on his head.

'Twenty thousand francs for a "short stay", as they call it at the Hôtel Beauséjour . . .'

Trying to appear unfazed, Jaja wiped her chubby hands on her apron. She didn't dare say a thing. She was completely flabbergasted.

And Sylvie, drained of blood, her features drawn, didn't look at anyone but just stared into space; she could see nothing ahead but the cruellest blows of fate.

'You can sit down,' Maigret barked.

She obeyed automatically.

'You too, Jaja . . . Wait . . . First find some clean glasses . . .'

Sylvie sat in the same place she had sat the previous day, when she had eaten with her dressing gown gaping open, her bare breasts just a few centimetres from her plate.

Jaja placed a bottle and some glasses on the table and sat down on the very edge of her seat.

'Right then, girls, I'm waiting . . .'

The smoke from his pipe rose slowly to the rectangular window, which now had a bluish tinge, as the sun no longer penetrated. Jaja looked at Sylvie . . .

And the latter continued to stare at nothing, absent or subdued.

'I'm waiting . . .'

He could have said it a hundred times, waited ten years. The only sound was Jaja's sigh as she buried her chin in her bosom:

'My God . . . If only I knew . . .'

As for Maigret, he could barely contain himself. He got up. He paced up and down. He grumbled:

'I should really . . .'

The statue infuriated him. Once, twice, three times he walked past Sylvie, who remained frozen.

'I have plenty of time . . . But . . .'

On the fourth occasion he couldn't take it any more. It was mechanical. His hand grabbed the young woman's shoulder and he wasn't aware how tightly he was gripping it.

She raised a hand in front of her face, like a little girl afraid of being hit.

'Well?'

She gave in, under the pain. She cried out, bursting into tears:

'You bully! . . . You filthy bully! . . . I'll say nothing . . . Nothing! . . . Nothing!'

It was making Jaja feel ill. Maigret, with a stubborn frown, let himself slide on to a chair. And Sylvie continued crying without covering her face, without wiping her eyes, crying as much from rage as from pain.

'Nothing!' she repeated in her mechanical fashion between two sobs.

The door of the bar opened – something that happened no more than ten times a day. A customer sat at the zinc counter and turned the handle on the fruit machine.

7. The Order

Maigret stood up impatiently and, to forestall any potential trick on the part of the two women – the customer could be a messenger from Joseph, for example – he decided to go into the bar himself.

'What do you want?'

The man seemed so taken aback that, in spite of his bad mood, Maigret almost burst out laughing. He was a middle-aged fellow, dull complexion, grey hair, who no doubt had crept furtively through the sidestreets in pursuit of some dream of unbridled sex, only to have the surly Maigret pop up behind the bar!

'A bock . . .' he stammered, letting go of the slot-machine handle.

Behind the curtain, the inspector could see the two women in a huddle. Jaja was asking questions, and Sylvie was replying wearily.

'There's no beer!'

At least, Maigret couldn't see any within reach!

'Then whatever you like . . . A port maybe . . .'

Maigret poured some liquid or other in the first glass he could find. The man barely sipped it.

'How much?'

'Two francs.'

Maigret alternately observed the street, still bathed in

warm sunshine, the small bar opposite, where he could see moving shapes, and the back room, where Jaja had sat down again.

The customer left, wondering what sort of place he had landed up in, and Maigret returned to the back room and sat down astride his chair.

Jaja's demeanour had changed somewhat. Earlier, she had looked worried, and it was obvious she didn't know what to think. Now, her anxiety seemed more focused. She looked at Sylvie pensively, a look of pity with a barb of rancour. She seemed to be saying: 'It's a fine mess that you have got yourself into! It won't be easy to find a way out of it!'

She said out loud:

'You know, inspector . . . Men can be strange . . .'

Her words lacked conviction, and she knew it. As did Sylvie, who shrugged her shoulders.

'He saw her at the funeral this morning and he must have desired her . . . He is so rich that . . .'

Maigret sighed, lit another pipe and let his gaze wander to the window.

There was an ominous atmosphere in the room. Sylvie was keeping her mouth shut for fear of making things worse. She wasn't crying, wasn't moving, just waiting for who knows what.

Only the small alarm clock kept working, pushing its black hands, which seemed too heavy for it, laboriously round its pale clock face.

Tick tock, tick tock, tick tock . . .

Jaja was not made for such dramas. She got up and went to fetch a bottle of alcohol from the cupboard. As if nothing were going on, she filled three glasses and slid one across to Maigret, another to Sylvie, without saying a word.

The twenty thousand francs were still on the table, next to the handbag.

Tick tock, tick . . .

And so it went on, for an hour and a half! An hour and a half of silence, interspersed only by Jaja's sighs. As she drank, her eyes became glassy.

Occasionally some children would play and shout out in the street. At other times there was the insistent sound of a tram bell somewhere in the distance. The door of the bar opened. An Arab poked his head through the gap and called out:

'Peanuts?'

He waited a moment then, receiving no response, closed the door again and left.

It was six o'clock before the door opened again, and this time the stir it created in the back room suggested that this was the moment Maigret had been waiting for. Jaja was about to get up to run to the bar, but a look from him stopped her in her tracks. Sylvie turned her head away, feigning indifference.

The second door opened. Joseph came in. He saw Maigret's back first of all, then the table, the glasses, the bottle, the open handbag, the banknotes.

The inspector turned round slowly, and the new arrival, quite motionless, merely muttered:

'Damn!'

'Close the door . . . Take a seat . . .'

The waiter closed the door, but he didn't sit. He scowled,

looked annoyed, but he didn't lose his cool. Quite the opposite: he went up to Jaja and kissed her on the forehead.

'Hello . . .'

Then he did the same to Sylvie, who didn't raise her head.

'What's going on?'

From that moment Maigret realized that he was on the wrong track. But, as always in such situations, he pressed on even more stubbornly as he felt himself become more entangled.

'Where have you come from?'

'Guess!'

And he took a wallet from his pocket and took out a small card, which he handed to Maigret. It was an identity card, the sort given to foreigners resident in France.

'I was late . . . I went to renew it at the Préfecture . . .'

The card did indeed bear today's date, the name: 'Joseph Ambrosini, born Milan, profession: hotel employee'.

'Did you meet Harry Brown?'

'Me?'

'Did you meet him for the first time last Tuesday or Wednesday?'

Joseph looked at him, smiling, as if to say: 'What are you on about?'

'Come on, Ambrosini. I assume you will not deny that you are Sylvie's lover . . .'

'Depends what you mean by that . . . Something happened . . .'

'No! No! You are what is euphemistically known as her "protector" . . .'

Poor Jaja! She had never been so unhappy in her life. The alcohol was skewing her view of the situation. Every now and again she opened her mouth to try to make some conciliatory remark, and it was obvious what she was trying to say: 'Come on, everyone! Let's make up! Is it really worth all this strife? Let's all have a drink together and . . .'

As for Joseph, it was obvious that this wasn't his first run-in with the police. He was guarded. He remained cool, didn't overplay his hand.

'Your information is incorrect . . .'

'And I suppose you don't know anything about these twenty thousand francs?'

'I guess Sylvie must have earned it . . . She's a good-looking girl . . .'

'Enough!'

Maigret was on his feet again. He was pacing up and down in the small room. Sylvie was looking at her feet. Joseph, however, never lowered his gaze.

'Will you have something?' asked Jaja, for whom this was just another opportunity to have a drink.

Maigret couldn't quite make his mind up. He stood there for a while, in front of the alarm clock, which was showing a quarter past six. When he turned round, he said:

'Very well! You two will accompany me . . . I am arresting you!'

Ambrosini didn't flinch, but merely murmured, with the faintest hint of irony:

'As you wish!'

The inspector put the twenty thousand-franc notes in his pocket and handed Sylvie her hat and bag.

'Do I need to cuff you, or will you give me your word . . .'

'I won't try to escape. Let's go!'

Jaja was sobbing in Sylvie's arms. The latter was trying to free herself. They had great trouble preventing the fat woman from following the group into the street.

Lights were coming on. It was that mild hour of the day again. They passed near the street where the Hôtel Beauséjour was. But Joseph didn't glance in that direction.

At the police station the day shift was clocking off. The secretary was in a hurry to get Maigret to sign the forms.

'Lock them up separately . . . I will probably come by this evening to see them . . .'

Sylvie had sat on a bench at the back of the office. Joseph was rolling up a cigarette, which a uniformed officer snatched from his hands.

And Maigret went off without saying a word, turning only once towards Sylvie, who wasn't looking at him. He shrugged and muttered:

'Too bad!'

Wedged into his seat, he didn't even notice that the bus had become crowded and an old woman was standing next to him. Turned towards the window, watching the headlights of the cars as they swept past, he smoked furiously. The old lady had to bend over and murmur:

'Excuse me, sir . . .'

He looked like he was emerging from a dream. He jumped to his feet, not knowing where to tip out his burning embers, and was in such a kerfuffle that the young couple behind him burst out laughing.

At seven thirty he went in through the revolving door of the Provençal and found Inspector Boutigues sitting in an armchair in the lobby, where he was chatting to the manager.

'Well?'

'He's upstairs . . .' replied Boutigues, who seemed troubled.

'Did you tell him . . . ?'

'Yes . . . He didn't seem surprised . . . I was expecting more of a protest . . .'

The manager lingered a while to ask a question, but as soon as he opened his mouth Maigret hurried to the lift.

'Shall I wait for you?' Boutigues called after him.

'If you like . . .'

He knew well this mental state he had been in for the last two or three hours! And he was in a rage, as he always was in such situations! But that didn't mean he was incapable of reacting . . .

That confused feeling of making a blunder . . . He had had that feeling since he had met Sylvie at the door of the hotel . . .

And yet something was impelling him to forge ahead!

Worse than that, he was charging forwards all the more passionately since he wanted to persuade himself that he was right!

The lift went up smoothly on well-oiled wheels. And Maigret repeated to himself the order he'd been given:

'No dramas!'

That's why he was in Antibes! To prevent any dramas, any scandal!

At any other time he would have gone into Brown's suite without his pipe. Now he lit it deliberately. He knocked on the door and went straight in. The scene was exactly the same as the day before:

Brown pacing up and down, impeccably dressed, instructing his secretary, answering the telephone and trying to dictate a cable to Sydney.

'May I see you for a moment?'

No sign of anxiety! Here was a man completely at ease in all the situations life threw at him. He didn't even falter that morning while seeing his father off in such extraordinary circumstances. The presence of the four women didn't seem to unsettle him in the slightest.

And that afternoon, coming out of that shady hotel, he didn't seem at all bothered. He didn't even flinch.

He continued with his dictation. At the same time he placed a box of cigars on the pedestal table opposite Maigret and pushed the electric bell.

'Take the telephone into the bedroom, James.'

And to the butler who came in:

'A whisky!'

How much of this attitude was posturing and how much was real?

'A good education,' mused Maigret. 'He must have gone to Oxford or Cambridge . . .'

It was an old grudge by a former student of Collège Stanislas. One tempered by a certain admiration.

'Take your typewriter with you, please, mademoiselle.'

But no! Brown saw that the typist was encumbered by her notepad and pencils. He took the heavy typewriter himself and carried it into the adjoining room, then locked the door.

Then he waited for the butler to bring the whisky and indicated that the drink should be served to Maigret.

Only when they were alone did he pull out his wallet from his pocket and take from it a stamped piece of paper which he glanced at before handing to the inspector.

'Read this . . . Do you understand English?'

'Not very well.'

'It's the piece of paper I paid twenty thousand francs for this afternoon at the Hôtel Beauséjour.'

He sat down, a gesture of relaxation.

'I should first of all explain a few small things . . . Do you know Australia at all? . . . A shame . . . My father, before he got married, owned a very large estate . . . as large as a French *département* . . . After his marriage, he was the largest sheep breeder in Australia, because my mother brought an estate of comparable size as her dowry . . .'

Harry Brown spoke slowly, taking great care not to use superfluous words, to be clear.

'Are you a Protestant?' Maigret asked.

'My whole family are. And my mother's too!'

He wanted to continue. Maigret interrupted him:

'Your father didn't study in Europe, did he?'

'No! It wasn't the done thing at the time . . . He only came here after his marriage . . . Five years after, when he already had three children . . .'

Too bad if Maigret had got it wrong! In his mind's eye he saw all this as a set of images: he sketched out a mansion, huge but austere, in the middle of the estate. And serious people who resembled Presbyterian ministers.

William Brown, who took over from his father, got married, had children and occupied himself purely with running the business . . .

'One day he had to come to Europe, because of a trial . . .'

'On his own?'

'Yes, he came on his own!'

It was so simple! Paris! London! Berlin! The Côte d'Azur! And Brown realized that a man with his colossal fortune in this glittering new world, full of temptations, was like a king!

'And he never returned home!' Maigret sighed.

'No! He wanted to . . .'

The trial dragged on. The people with whom the sheep farmer was in contact took him out to places where he could have fun. He met women there.

'For two years he kept postponing his return . . .'

'Who was running the business back home?'

'My mother . . . And her brother . . . We received letters from locals who said . . .'

That was enough! Maigret had all the information he needed. Brown, who had known nothing but his country estate, his sheep, his neighbours and church ministers, became a wild hedonist, indulging in pleasures he hadn't even known existed until then . . .

He kept putting back his return to Australia . . . He made sure that the trial dragged on even longer . . . And once the trial was concluded, he found new excuses to stay here . . .

He had bought a yacht . . . He was one of only a few

dozen people who could buy anything, who could have anything they desired . . .

'Your mother and uncle finally placed him under legal guardianship?'

Back home, they were defending their interests! They had legal rulings! And one day, in Nice or Monte Carlo, William Brown woke up to find that his entire fortune consisted of a subsistence pension!

'He continued to run up debts for a while, and we paid them off . . .' said Harry.

'Then you stopped paying?'

'Excuse me! I continued to pay an allowance of five thousand francs a month . . .'

Maigret sensed that he hadn't got to the bottom of things yet. He felt a vague unease that he expressed in a forthright question:

'What did you come to discuss with your father, a few days before he died?'

Maigret scrutinized Brown carefully, but in vain. He was unperturbed and replied in his usual straightforward fashion:

'Despite everything, he still had rights, didn't he? . . . He fought the ruling for fifteen years . . . It was a big trial back home . . . Five lawyers who worked on this case exclusively . . . And while it went on we were in a state of limbo that prevented us from carrying out certain large undertakings . . .'

'One moment . . . On one side, your father, living all alone in France and represented by lawyers in Australia who defended his interests.'

'Lawyers of dubious reputation . . .'

'Quite! . . . In the other camp, your mother, your uncle, your two brothers and you.'

'Yes!' He spoke in English.

'And what were you offering your father to drop out of circulation completely?'

'A million!'

'In other words, he would be better off, since the pension you paid him was worth less than the interest on that lump sum, properly invested . . . Why would he say no?'

'To get under our skin!'

Harry said this in a soft voice. He probably didn't know that the words sounded somewhat incongruous in his mouth.

'He was obsessed . . . He wouldn't leave us in peace . . .'

'So he said no . . .'

'Yes! And he told me that he had made arrangements so that, even after his death, our problems would continue . . .'

'What sort of problems?'

'The trial! Back home, it was causing a lot of damage . . .'

Was there any need for further explanation? He only needed to imagine the Liberty Bar, Jaja, a half-naked Sylvie, William bringing provisions . . . Or the villa and the two Martini women, the young one and the old one, and the old car in which he drove them to the market . . .

Then to look at Harry Brown, who represented the opposing principles, order, virtue, justice, with his slicked-back hair, his smart suit, his calm composure, his somewhat distant politeness, his secretaries . . .

'To get under our skin!'

William became more alive to him now! For so long

of the same mould as his son, as all the others *back home*, he had made a break with order, virtue and good breeding . . .

He had become the enemy and had purely and simply been dismissed from the family . . .

He dug in, of course. He knew that he would not win the case! He knew that he would henceforth always be the outcast!

But he would get under their skin!

He would be capable of anything to do that – get under the skin of his wife, his brother-in-law, his children, who had disowned him, who continued to work to make money, always more money . . .

'With his death,' Harry calmly explained, 'the trial would fizzle out, and all the problems and all the scandalous stories that the nasty people back home fed upon . . .'

'Obviously!'

'So he drew up a will . . . He couldn't disinherit his wife and children . . . But he could dispose of part of his fortune . . . And do you know to whom he bequeathed it? . . . Four women . . .'

Maigret almost burst out laughing. In any case, he couldn't prevent himself smiling at the thought of the two Martinis, mother and daughter, and Jaja and Sylvie arriving in Australia to defend their rights . . .

'Is that the will that you have in your hand?'

It was a full document, properly drawn up in the presence of a notary.

'That's what my father was referring to when he said that, even after his death, this story would not go away . . .'

'Do you know the terms of the will?'

'As late as this morning I knew nothing at all . . . When I returned to the Provençal, after the funeral, there was a man waiting for me . . .'

'Was his name Joseph?'

'Some sort of waiter . . . He showed me a copy . . . He told me that, if I wanted to buy the original, I only had to go to a hotel in Cannes and bring twenty thousand francs . . . This type of person is not in the habit of lying . . .'

Maigret had adopted a stern demeanour.

'In other words, you were prepared to destroy a will! There was even an attempt . . .'

Brown looked just as unperturbed as before.

'I know what I'm doing!' he said calmly. 'And I know that these women are . . .'

He stood up, glanced at Maigret's full glass.

'You're not drinking?'

'No, thank you.'

'I'm sure any court would recognize . . .'

'That the gang back home must come out on top . . .'

What had impelled Maigret to say that? The desire to blunder onwards and be damned?

Harry Brown didn't turn a hair. Walking to the door of the bedroom, where the tapping of the typewriter continued unabated, he said:

'The document is intact . . . I leave it with you . . . I'll stay here until . . .'

The door opened and the secretary announced:

'It's London on the line . . .'

He had the phone in his hand. Brown grabbed it and started talking volubly in English.

Maigret took the opportunity to leave, with the will. He pressed the lift button, but to no effect, so he ended up taking the stairs, repeating to himself as he descended:

'No dramas!'

Downstairs, Inspector Boutigues was drinking port with the manager. Two large cut-crystal tasting glasses. And the bottle close to hand!

8. *The Four Heirs*

Boutigues skipped along at Maigret's side, and they had barely gone twenty metres when he announced:

'I've just made a discovery! . . . I've known the manager here for ages, and he oversees the Hôtel du Cap, in Cap Ferrat, which is part of the same chain . . .'

They had just left the Provençal. Before them, in the dark, the sea was nothing but a pool of black ink with barely a ripple on it.

To the right, the lights of Cannes. To the left, those of Nice. And Boutigues pointed with his hand to the darkness beyond these swarms of fireflies.

'Do you know Cap Ferrat? . . . Between Nice and Monte Carlo . . .'

Maigret did. He had now more or less worked out the Côte d'Azur: one long boulevard starting in Cannes and ending in Menton, a boulevard sixty kilometres long, with villas and the occasional casino, a handful of luxury hotels . . .

The famous blue sea . . . The mountains . . . And all the attractions promised by the tourist guides: orange trees, mimosas, sun, palm trees, stone pines, tennis, golf, tea rooms and American bars . . .

'And what did you discover?'

'Yes, well. Harry Brown has a mistress on the Côte! The manager has spotted her numerous times in Cap Ferrat, where he visits her . . . A woman around thirty, widowed or divorced, very proper, by all accounts, whom he has set up in a villa . . .'

Was Maigret listening? He was looking at the impressive night-time panorama with a grumpy expression. Boutigues continued:

'He goes to see her about once a month . . . And it's a running joke at the Hôtel du Cap because he goes through a whole rigmarole to attempt to hide his affair . . . To the extent that, whenever he spends the night with her, he comes back in via the service stairs and then makes out that he's not been out at all . . .'

'Very amusing!' said Maigret, so half-heartedly that Boutigues felt quite discouraged.

'Do you want him put under surveillance?'

'No . . . yes . . .'

'Are you going to pay a visit to the lady in Cap Ferrat?'

Maigret didn't know! He couldn't think of three dozen things at the same time, and at the moment he wasn't thinking about Harry Brown, but about William. In Place Macé he lightly squeezed his companion's hand and hopped into a taxi.

'Follow the Cap d'Antibes road. I'll tell you where to stop.'

And he repeated to himself, all alone in the back of the taxi:

'William Brown was murdered!'

The small gate, the gravel path, then the bell, an electric light coming on above the door, footsteps in the hall, the door opening . . .

'It's you,' Gina Martini sighed when she recognized the inspector and then stepped back to allow him to enter.

A man's voice could be heard in the living room.

'Come in . . . Allow me to explain . . .'

The man was standing up, with a notebook in his hand, and half the old woman's body had disappeared inside a cupboard.

'Monsieur Petitfils . . . We asked him to come in order to . . .'

Monsieur Petitfils was a thin man with a long, drooping moustache and tired-looking eyes.

'He is the manager of one of the principal letting agencies for villas . . . We called him for some advice and . . .'

Still that same smell of musk. The two women had taken off their mourning clothes and were wearing dressing gowns and slippers.

The place was a mess. Was the light even dimmer than usual? Everything looked a dull grey. The old woman emerged from her cupboard, greeted Maigret and explained:

'Since I saw those two women at the funeral, I haven't felt at ease . . . So I approached Monsieur Petitfils to ask his advice . . . He agrees with me that it would be best to draw up an inventory . . .'

'An inventory of what?'

'Of the objects that belonged to us and those that belonged to William . . . We have been at it since two o'clock this afternoon . . .'

That much was clear! There were piles of linen on the tables, disparate objects scattered on the ground, stacks of books, more linen in baskets . . .

And Monsieur Petitfils took some notes and put crosses next to certain objects on his list.

What had Maigret come here for? It wasn't Brown's villa any more, so there was no point in looking for his memory here. They were clearing out the cupboards, the drawers, piling everything up, sorting, logging.

'As for the stove, that has always belonged to me,' said the old woman. 'I had it twenty years ago, in my lodgings in Toulouse.'

'Can I offer you anything, inspector?' asked Gina.

There was one dirty glass: that of the businessman. As he wrote his notes, he was smoking one of Brown's cigars.

'No, thank you . . . I just came by to say . . .'

To say what?

'. . . that I hope to arrest the murderer tomorrow . . .'

'Already?'

They weren't that interested. Instead, the old woman asked him:

'You must have been to see the son, is that right? . . . What did he say? . . . What is he planning to do? . . . Does he intend to come and take everything away from us?'

'I don't know . . . I don't think so . . .'

'It would be a disgrace! People as rich as they are! But then they are usually the ones who . . .'

The old woman was in a genuine state. The worry was eating away at her. She looked at all the old stuff lying about the room and felt a terrible anguish at the thought of losing it.

And Maigret had his hand on his wallet. All he had to do was open it, take out a little slip of paper and show it to the two women . . .

Would they dance for joy? Would the joy be too much for the old woman and be the end of her?

Millions and millions! Millions they couldn't yet get their hands on, of course, and that they would have to go to Australia to acquire by means of legal action!

But they would go! He could picture them sailing off, disembarking from the steamship over there with their noses in the air.

It wouldn't be Monsieur Petitfils whose services they would call on, but those of notaries, lawyers, barristers . . .

'I'll let you get on . . . I'll come by and see you tomorrow . . .'

His taxi was waiting at the gate. He sat down without giving an address, and the driver waited, holding the door open.

'Cannes . . .' Maigret finally said.

And it was the same thoughts that passed through his mind:

'Brown was murdered!'

'No dramas!'

Damn Brown! If the wound had been in his chest, you could have believed that he killed himself to spite everyone. But you don't stab yourself in the back, for heaven's sake!

He was no longer the one who intrigued Maigret. The

inspector felt that he knew him as well as if he had been a lifelong friend.

First of all, William in Australia . . . A rich, well-brought-up boy, a little shy, living with his parents, marrying someone suitable when the time comes and having children . . .

This Brown was fairly similar to Brown Junior . . . He might experience some vague melancholy or troubling desires, but he no doubt put them down to a passing phase and managed to get them out of his system.

The same William in Europe . . . The dykes finally bursting . . . He could no longer keep everything repressed . . . He was driven crazy by all the possibilities on offer to him . . .

And he became a regular on this boulevard that runs from Cannes to Menton . . . A yacht in Cannes . . . Baccarat games in Nice . . . The lot! . . . And an overwhelming apathy at the thought of returning *back home* . . .

'Next month, maybe . . .'

And the following month it was exactly the same!

So they cut off his allowance. The brother-in-law kept an eye on things. All the Brown family and all their hangers-on defended themselves!

He was incapable of leaving his boulevard, the sweet atmosphere of the Côte d'Azur, the indulgence, the easiness . . .

No more yacht. A small villa . . .

In the world of women he had to lower his standards too, and so he ended up with Gina Martini.

A certain disgust . . . A need for disorder and listlessness . . . The villa at Cap d'Antibes is still too bourgeois . . .

He discovered the Liberty Bar . . . Jaja . . . Sylvie . . .

And he continued the legal action, back home, against the Browns who had stayed on the rails, to get under their skin . . . He used his will to make sure he continued to do so after his death . . . Whether he was right or wrong was of no concern to Maigret. Yet the inspector couldn't help comparing the father with the son, Harry Brown, so proper and self-possessed, who knew how to keep things in perspective.

Harry didn't like mess! Nevertheless, Harry had troubling needs.

And he installed a mistress in Cap Ferrat . . . A very respectable, well-mannered mistress, a widow or divorcee, discreet . . .

Even at his hotel no one was supposed to know that he stayed out all night!

Order . . . Mess . . . Order . . . Mess . . .

Maigret was the umpire, as he had the famous will in his pocket!

He could at any moment allow four women to enter the fray!

What a singularly extraordinary picture that would make: these four women of William Brown arriving over there. Jaja with her sensitive feet, her swollen ankles, her sagging breasts . . . Sylvie, who in private can bear to wear nothing but a dressing gown over her skinny body . . .

Then the older Martini, with her cheeks caked in make-up! The younger one with her distinctive smell of musk.

They drove along the famous boulevard. The lights of Cannes were visible ahead.

'No dramas!'

The taxi pulled up in front of the Ambassadeurs, and the driver asked:

'Where do you want me to take you?'

'Nowhere! Here's fine.'

Maigret paid. The casino was lit up. A number of chauffeur-driven cars were arriving, for it was nearly nine in the evening.

And twelve casinos were similarly lighting up along the stretch between Cannes and Menton! And hundreds of luxury cars . . .

Maigret went on foot to the small sidestreet, where he found the Liberty Bar closed. No lights on. No light anywhere except that of the streetlamp shining through the window, throwing a murky light on the zinc counter-top and the fruit machine.

He knocked and was amazed at the din it made in the small street. Straight away the door behind him opened, the one to the bar across the street. The waiter called out to Maigret.

'Are you looking for Jaja?'

'Yes.'

'Who should I say . . . ?'

'The inspector.'

'In that case, I have a message for you . . . Jaja will be back in a few minutes . . . She asked me to tell you to wait . . . If you'd like to come in . . .'

'No, thank you.'

He was happier pacing up and down. He didn't like the look of the handful of customers in the bar across the street. A window opened somewhere. A woman, who had heard the noise, asked timidly:

'Is that you, Jean?'

'No!'

And Maigret, who had paced the street from one end to the other, repeated to himself:

'Above all, we need to find out who killed William!'

Ten o'clock . . . Jaja still hadn't arrived . . . Each time he heard footsteps he quivered in anticipation that his wait was coming to an end . . . But it wasn't her . . .

His horizon was a badly paved street fifty metres long and two metres wide; the illuminated window of one bar, the dark gloom of the other . . .

And the old, teetering buildings, their windows that weren't even rectangular any more.

Maigret went into the bar across the street.

'Did she say where she was going?'

'No! Would you like something to drink?'

And the customers, who had been told who he was, looked at him from head to toe!

'No, thank you!'

He started walking again, as far as the corner of the street, the border between this shady world and the brightly lit quayside, buzzing with everyday life.

Ten thirty . . . Eleven o'clock . . . The first café round the corner was called Harry's Bar. That's where Maigret had phoned from that afternoon when he was with Sylvie. He went in and made for the cabin.

'Could you give me the police? . . . Hello! . . . Police? . . . This is Detective Chief Inspector Maigret . . . Have

the two persons I delivered to you earlier received any
visitors?'

'Yes . . . A large woman . . .'

'Whom did she see?'

'First the man . . . Then the woman . . . We weren't sure
what to do . . . You didn't leave any instructions . . .'

'How long ago?'

'A good hour and a half . . . She brought cigarettes and
cakes . . .'

Maigret hung up, worried. Then, without pausing for
breath, he asked for the Provençal.

'Hello! . . . This is the police . . . Yes, the inspector you
saw earlier . . . Could you tell me whether Monsieur
Brown has received any visitors?'

'A quarter of an hour ago . . . A woman . . . Somewhat
badly dressed . . .'

'Where was he?'

'He was having a meal in the dining room . . . He took
her up to his room . . .'

'Has she gone?'

'She came down just as you rang.'

'Very fat, quite common-looking?'

'That's the one.'

'Was she in a taxi?'

'No . . . She left on foot . . .'

Maigret hung up, sat down in the bar and ordered sauer-
kraut and beer.

Jaja saw Sylvie and Joseph . . . She was given a message
for Harry Brown . . . She is coming back by bus, which
would take half an hour . . .

He ate and read the newspaper he found lying on the table. There was an item about two lovers who had committed suicide in Bandol. The man was married, in Czechoslovakia.

'Would you like some vegetables?'

'No, thank you! What do I owe you? . . . No, wait! . . . Another beer – stout . . .'

And five minutes later he was walking down the street again, past the darkened window of the Liberty Bar.

The curtain would be going up at the casino now. Gala evening. Opera. Dance. Supper. Dancing. Roulette and baccarat . . .

Along the whole sixty kilometres. Hundreds of women would be watching the diners. Hundreds of croupiers would be watching the gamblers! And hundreds of gigolos, dancers and waiters would be watching the women . . .

And then hundreds of businessmen, like Monsieur Petit-fils, with their lists of villas for sale or rent, watching the winter visitors . . .

Here and there – in Cannes, Nice or Monte Carlo – a part of town less well lit than the others, with narrow sidestreets, odd, run-down buildings, shadows flitting along the walls, old women and youths, fruit machines and back rooms . . .

Still no Jaja! Ten times Maigret started when he heard footsteps. In the end he couldn't face walking in front of the bar across the road, where the waiter was watching with amusement.

And during this time, thousands, tens of thousands, of sheep would be munching the Browns' grass on the

Browns' estate tended by the Browns' shepherds . . . Tens of thousands of sheep about to be sheared – because it would be daytime now in the antipodes – the wool loaded on to wagons and shipped in huge cargos . . .

And the sailors, ship's officers, captains . . .

And all these ships coming to Europe, the officers checking the thermometers (to ensure the optimum temperature for the cargo), and the brokers in Amsterdam, London, Liverpool, Le Havre, discussing the price . . .

And Harry Brown, at the Provençal, receiving cables from his brothers, his uncle and telephoning his agents . . .

When he was looking through the paper earlier, Maigret had read:

The Commander of the Faithful, the leader of Islam, has married his daughter to Prince . . .

Followed by:

Great celebrations in India, Persia, Afghanistan . . .

And then:

A large dinner was mounted in Nice, at the Palais de la Méditerranée, where the eye-catching . . .

The daughter of the high priest getting married in Nice . . . A wedding on the sixty-odd-kilometre boulevard while back home hundreds of thousands of people . . .

But still no Jaja! Maigret knew every paving slab and

every house front on the street. A little girl with her hair in pigtails was doing her homework next to her window.

Had the bus had an accident? Did Jaja have to go somewhere else? Was she running away?

Pressing his forehead to the window of the bar, Maigret could see the cat licking its paws.

And more snippets remembered from the newspaper:

It is reported from the Côte d'Azur that S. M., the king of . . . , has arrived at his property in Cap Ferrat, accompanied by . . .

News of the arrest of M. Graphopoulos, who was apprehended in a baccarat room having just won more than five hundred thousand francs by using a false card shoe . . .

Then a short sentence:

The deputy director of police is compromised.

Good grief! If William Brown succumbed, is some poor guy on two thousand francs a month supposed to be a hero?

Maigret was furious. He had had enough of waiting! Above all, he had had enough of the atmosphere of this place, which rubbed him up the wrong way.

Why had he been given a ridiculous order like: 'No dramas'?

No dramas? . . . What if he produced a will, a genuine, incontestable will? . . . And sent the four women off over there?

Footsteps . . . He didn't even turn round! . . . A few

moments later, a key turned in a lock and a sickly voice sighed:

'Ah, there you are.'

It was Jaja. A tired Jaja, whose hand shook as it held the key. A Jaja dressed to the nines, mauve overcoat and oxblood-red shoes.

'Come in . . . Wait . . . I'll turn the lights on . . .'

The cat purred as it rubbed against her swollen legs. She searched for the light switch.

'When I think about poor Sylvie . . .'

Finally, she managed to turn on the light. Now they could see. The waiter in the café across the street had his ugly face glued to the window.

'Come in, please . . . I'm exhausted . . . All this emotion . . .'

And the door to the back room opened. Jaja went straight to the fire, which was burning red, half closed the damper, moved a pot.

'Sit down, inspector . . . Just give me time to change and I'll be with you . . .'

She hadn't yet looked him in the face. With her back turned to Maigret, she repeated:

'Poor Sylvie . . .'

And she climbed the stairs to the mezzanine and continued talking as she changed, her voice a little higher-pitched.

'A good girl . . . If she had wanted to be. But they are the ones who always end up paying the price for others . . . I'd told her . . .'

Maigret had sat down in front of the table, where there were some leftover cheese, pâté de tête, sardines.

Above his head he could hear the sound of Jaja taking off her shoes and dragging some slippers towards her.

Then the jig she danced to get her trousers off without sitting down.

9. Chatter

'All this stress. It's making my feet swell up . . .'

Jaja had stopped walking around and had sat down. She had her shoes off and was massaging her painful feet, with a mechanical movement, as she spoke.

She was speaking loudly, because she thought Maigret was downstairs, so she was surprised to see him appear at the top of the staircase.

'Ah, there you are . . . Don't mind the mess . . . There's just so much going on . . .'

Maigret would be hard put to say why he had come upstairs. As he had sat listening to his companion, it suddenly occurred to him that he hadn't yet seen the mezzanine.

Now he was standing at the top of the stairs. Jaja continued to rub her feet and she carried on talking, even more volubly:

'Have I even eaten? . . . I don't think so . . . It's turned me inside out seeing Sylvie in that place . . .'

She had slipped on a dressing gown but unlike Sylvie she wore it over her underwear, which was bright pink. A very short slip, trimmed with lace, which contrasted with her flabby white skin.

The bed was unmade. Maigret thought that, if anyone could see him now, he would have difficulty making them believe that he was here just to talk.

An ordinary-looking room, less poor than one might have thought. A mahogany bed, very bourgeois. A round table. A chest of drawers. On the other hand, the slop bucket was in the middle of the room and the table was covered with make-up, dirty tissues and pots of cream.

Jaja sighed as she finally pulled her slippers on.

'I wonder how it will all turn out.'

'Did William sleep here when he . . .'

'This is the only room I have, apart from the two downstairs . . .'

In the corner, there was a divan, its velour upholstery well worn.

'Did he sleep on the divan?'

'It varied . . . Sometimes it was me . . .'

'And Sylvie?'

'With me . . .'

The ceiling was so low that Maigret touched it with the top of his hat. The window was narrow, covered by a curtain in green velour. The electric lamp had no shade.

It didn't require great powers of imagination to picture normal life in this room: William and Jaja coming upstairs, usually drunk, then Sylvie following on and slipping in next to the fat woman . . .

But the mornings? . . . With the bright light from outside?

Jaja had never been so chatty. She spoke in a doleful voice, as if looking for pity.

'I bet this all makes me ill . . . Yes! I can feel it . . . Just like three years ago, when the sailors had a fight right outside my house . . . One of them got cut by a razor and . . .'

She stood up. She looked around her, searching for something, then forgot what it was she was looking for.

'Have you eaten? . . . Come . . . We'll grab a bite to eat . . .'

Maigret went first down the stairs, watched her head to the stove, shovel in some coal, stir a pot with a spoon.

'When I'm on my own I don't feel up to cooking . . . And when I think about where Sylvie is at this moment . . .'

'Tell me, Jaja . . .'

'What?'

'What did Sylvie say to you this afternoon when I was in the bar serving a customer?'

'Oh yes! . . . I asked her about the twenty grand . . . She told me she didn't know, it was some scheme of Joseph's . . .'

'And this evening?'

'This evening what?'

'At the police station . . .'

'The same thing . . . She was wondering what Joseph had been cooking up . . .'

'Has she been with this Joseph for long?'

'She's with him but not with him . . . They don't live together . . . She met him somewhere, probably at the races, in any case not here . . . He said he could be of use to her, bring her clients . . . Obviously, the line he is in! . . . He's got good manners . . . But even so, I've never liked him . . .'

There were some leftover lentils in a pot, and Jaja tipped them on to a plate.

'Want some? . . . No? . . . Help yourself to a drink . . . I don't feel up to doing anything . . . Is the front door closed?'

Maigret was straddling his chair, just like he had that afternoon. He watched her eat. He listened to her speak.

'You know, those people, especially the ones from the casinos, are too tricky for the likes of us . . . And throughout history it's always been the woman who gets taken in . . . If Sylvie had listened to me . . .'

'What did Joseph ask you to do this evening?'

At first she seemed not to understand but looked at Maigret with her mouth full.

'Ah yes! . . . The son . . .'

'What did you go to tell him?'

'To ask him to arrange to get them released, otherwise . . .'

'Otherwise what?'

'Oh! I know you won't leave me in peace . . . But you'll see that I've never done you wrong . . . I do everything I can! . . . I've got nothing to hide.'

He guessed the reason for her volubility, her whining voice.

On the way home, Jaja had stopped off in a few bars, for Dutch courage!

'First off, it was me who held Sylvie back, who prevented her from getting too involved with Joseph . . . Then, when I found out just now that there was something . . .'

'Well?'

It was more comic than tragic. Still eating, she started to cry! It was a grotesque spectacle: this large woman in her mauve dressing gown crying like a baby into her plate of lentils.

'Don't try to rush me . . . Let me think! . . . If you think I've got anything to gain from this . . . Hang on! Give me a drink . . .'

'Later!'

'Give me a drink and I'll tell you everything . . .'

He gave in and poured her a small glass.

'What do you want to know? . . . What was I saying? . . . I saw the twenty thousand francs . . . Was it William who had them in his pocket?'

Maigret had to make an effort to keep a clear head for, little by little, things were getting disjointed, perhaps in part because of the atmosphere, but more because of Jaja's speech.

'William . . .'

Then suddenly he grasped it! Jaja had believed that the twenty thousand francs were stolen from Brown when he was murdered!

'Is that what you thought?'

'I don't know any more what I thought . . . Well, I'm not hungry any more . . . Do you have any cigarettes?'

'I only smoke a pipe.'

'There must be some somewhere . . . Sylvie always has some . . .'

And she searched all the drawers in vain.

'Do they still send them to Alsace?'

'Who? . . . What? . . . What are you talking about?'

'Women . . . What's it called again . . . That prison . . . It begins with "Hau" . . . In my time . . .'

'When you were in Paris?'

'Yes . . . Everyone was talking about it . . . They say it's so harsh all the prisoners try to kill themselves . . . And I read not so long ago in the paper that some are sent down for eighty years . . . I can't find any cigarettes . . . Sylvie must have taken them with her . . .'

'Is she frightened of going there?'

'Sylvie? . . . I've got no idea . . . I was just thinking about it on the bus on the way home . . . There was this old woman in front of me and . . .'

'Sit down . . .'

'Yes . . . Don't mind me . . . I'm shot . . . I'm all over the place . . . What were we talking about?'

And with an expression of anguish in her eyes she wiped her hand across her forehead, dislodging a lock of russet hair over her cheek.

'I'm sad . . . Give me something to drink, won't you?'

'When you've told me everything you know . . .'

'But I don't know anything! . . . What would I know? . . . I saw Sylvie first of all . . . Besides, there was a cop stood next to me, listening to what we were saying . . . I wanted to cry . . . Sylvie whispered to me as she hugged me that it was all Joseph's fault . . .'

'Then you went to see him?'

'Yes . . . I already told you . . . He sent me to Antibes to warn Brown that . . .'

She was trying to find the words. It was as if she were suffering sudden mental blanks, the way some drunks do. At those moments she looked at Maigret anxiously, as if she felt the need to cling to him.

'I don't know any more . . . Please don't torture me . . . I'm just a poor woman . . . I've always tried to please everyone . . .'

'No! Just wait . . .'

Maigret pulled her hand away from the glass she was trying to grasp because he could see the possibility of her passing out, dead drunk.

'Did Harry Brown receive you?'

'No . . . Yes . . . He told me that, if I ever crossed his path again, he'd have me locked up . . .'

Then suddenly, triumphantly:

'Hossegor! . . . No! . . . Hossegor's something else . . . It's a novel . . . Haguenau . . . That's it!'

It was the name of the prison she had been talking about earlier.

'They say that they're not allowed to talk . . . Do you think that's true?'

Maigret had never seen her as flaky as this. It was almost as if she were regressing to her childhood.

'Obviously, if Sylvie is an accomplice, she will go to . . .'

Then, more than ever, and more quickly, she started talking, and her cheeks were flushed with fever.

'But I learned a few things this evening . . . The twenty thousand francs, I now know it was Harry Brown, William's son, who brought them to pay for . . .'

'Pay for what?'

'Everything!'

And she looked at him triumphantly, defiantly.

'I'm not as stupid as I look . . . When the son realized that there was a will . . .'

'Excuse me! You know about the will?'

'William told us about it last month . . . All four of us were here . . .'

'You mean you, Sylvie and Joseph . . .'

'Yes . . . We opened a good bottle, because it was William's birthday . . . And we talked about all sorts of things . . . When he'd had a bit to drink, he told us things about Australia, his wife, his brother-in-law . . .'

'And what did William say?'

'That they would be stitched up when he died! He took the will out of his pocket and read us a part of it . . . Not all . . . He didn't want to read out the names of the two other women . . . He said that some day soon he would file it with a notary . . .'

'This was a month ago? Was it then that Joseph first met Harry Brown?'

'You never know with that one . . . He knew lots of people, because of his profession . . .'

'And you think he warned the son?'

'I'm not saying that! I'm not saying anything . . . Only, you can't help but think . . . Those rich people, they aren't any better than the rest of us . . . Suppose Joseph did tell him everything . . . William's son would have casually let slip that he'd be happy to lay hands on the will . . . But since William could easily write another one, it would be better if William were to die as well . . .'

Maigret had taken his eye off her. She poured herself another drink. He wasn't quick enough to stop her draining her glass. When she started talking again, he caught the foul smell of her drink-sodden breath full in the face.

She was bending forwards, coming close to him, adopting a mysterious, serious air.

'Die as well . . . Is that what I said? . . . So they discussed money . . . For twenty thousand francs . . . And maybe another twenty thousand paid later . . . You never know . . . These things aren't usually paid for in one instalment . . . As for Sylvie . . .'

'She knew nothing?'

'I swear to you that no one said anything to me! . . . Was that a knock at the door?'

She suddenly stiffened with fear. To reassure her, Maigret had to go to check. When he came back, he noticed that she had taken advantage of his absence and helped herself to another drink.

'I didn't say anything . . . I don't know anything . . . Do you understand? . . . I'm just a poor woman! A poor woman who has lost her husband and . . .'

And she burst into tears again; it was even more pitiful than before.

'As far as you know, Jaja, what did William do that day between two and five o'clock?'

She looked at him without replying and didn't stop crying. However, her sobs sounded a bit more fake.

'Sylvie left a few moments before him . . . Do you think that they maybe could have . . .'

'Who?'

'Sylvie and William . . .'

'Could have what?'

'I don't know! . . . Met up somewhere . . . Sylvie is pretty . . . She's young . . . And William . . .'

He didn't take his eyes off her. He feigned indifference:

'They met some place where Joseph could see them and do the deed . . .'

She said nothing. Rather, she looked at Maigret with a frown, as if she were making a huge effort to understand. And no wonder it was an effort. Her eyes were cloudy and her brain too was no doubt not quite in focus.

'Harry Brown, who is now fully informed concerning the will, orders the crime . . . Sylvie lures William to a suitable location . . . Joseph does the deed . . . Then Harry Brown is invited to give the money to Sylvie, in a hotel in Cannes . . .'

She didn't move. She listened, bewildered or simply drink-sodden.

'When Joseph was arrested, you let Harry know that unless he helps to free him he will talk . . .'

She literally cried out:

'That's right! . . . Yes, that's right . . .'

She had stood up. She was panting for breath. She seemed torn between the need to cry and the need to burst out laughing.

Suddenly, she grabbed her head with both hands in a convulsive gesture, pulled at her hair, stamped her feet.

'That's right! . . . And I . . . I . . .'

Maigret stayed sitting, watching her with some surprise. Was she about to break down, pass out?

'I . . . I . . .'

Outside the two doors there was only the gleam of the streetlamp and the sound of the waiter across the road closing the shutters. The trams had been silent for a while now.

'I don't want that, do you understand?' she yelped. 'No! . . . Not that! . . . I don't want that . . . It's not true . . . It's . . .'

'Jaja!'

But the sound of her name did little to calm her. She was at a pitch of frenzy, and as quickly as she had seized the bottle she bent down, picked something up and cried:

'Not Haguenau . . . It's not true . . . Sylvie didn't . . .'

Never in his working life had Maigret witnessed a scene as wretched as this. She had picked up a shard of glass and, as she talked, slashed her wrist, right over the artery . . .

Her eyes were bulging. She seemed mad.

'Haguenau . . . I . . . Not Sylvie!'

Blood spurted out just as Maigret managed to grab both her arms. It splashed on to his hand and tie.

For a few seconds Jaja, bewildered, out of control, looked at this flow of red blood that belonged to her. Then she went limp. Maigret held her up for a moment, then let her slide to the ground and tried to seal the artery with his finger.

He needed a tourniquet. He looked around frantically. There was an electric cable attached to a flat-iron. He pulled it out. All this time, the blood was flowing freely.

He went back to Jaja, who wasn't moving any more, wound the wire round her wrist and pulled it as tight as he could.

In the street the only light now was the gas lamp. The bar across the street was shut.

He went out, walking unsteadily, and felt the warm night air. He headed for the most brightly lit street, which was two hundred metres away.

From there he could see the floodlights of the casino, the cars, the chauffeurs in a group near the harbour. And the masts of yachts, barely stirring.

There was a policeman stationed in the middle of the crossroads.

'A doctor . . . To the Liberty Bar . . . Quickly . . .'

'Isn't that the bar that . . . ?'

'Yes! The bar that!' Maigret bellowed impatiently. 'Get a move on, for God's sake!'

10. *The Divan*

The two men climbed the stairs carefully, but the body was heavy, and the gangway was narrow, with the result that Jaja, who was being held by the shoulders and the feet, bent in two, sometimes bumped against the banister or the wall or scraped against the stairs.

The doctor, as he waited in turn to go upstairs, looked around him with curiosity, while Jaja moaned softly, like an unconscious animal. It was such a feeble moan, at such a strange pitch, that, although it filled the house, it was hard to pinpoint its source, as if it were uttered by a ventriloquist.

In the low room on the mezzanine Maigret made the bed then helped the police officers to lift Jaja up, for she was heavy and lifeless, even though she had the appearance of a large rag doll.

Was she conscious of all these peregrinations? Did she know where she was? Every now and again she opened her eyes, but she didn't look at anything or anyone. She continued to moan but did not screw up her face.

'Is she in much pain?' Maigret asked the doctor.

He was a kindly little old man, very meticulous, somewhat dismayed to find himself in such surroundings.

'She shouldn't be suffering any pain at all. She must be very delicate. Or maybe she's frightened . . .'

'Is she aware of what's going on?'

'By the look of her, I doubt it. Yet . . .'

'She's dead drunk!' sighed Maigret. 'I was just wondering whether the pain had sobered her up . . .'

The two policemen awaited instructions and they too looked around with curiosity. The curtains hadn't been closed. Maigret could see in the window opposite the pale halo of a face in the unilluminated room. He pulled down the blind and summoned one of the officers over from the corner.

'Bring me the woman that I had locked up earlier on. A certain Sylvie. But not the man.'

And to the other:

'Wait for me downstairs.'

The doctor had done all he could. Having applied haemostatic clips, he had stapled the artery closed. Now he was giving this fat woman, who was still groaning, a bored look. For appearances' sake, he took her pulse, felt her forehead and checked her hands.

'Come over here, doctor!' said Maigret, who was leaning his back against one corner of the room. Then, in a whisper:

'I'd be grateful if you would use this opportunity to give her a general examination . . . The vital organs, of course . . .'

'If you wish! If you wish!'

The little doctor was getting more and more bewildered, and he must have been wondering whether Maigret was related to Jaja. He selected some instruments from his case and, unhurriedly but with no great conviction, started to take her blood pressure.

Not liking what he found, he checked it three times in all, then bent over her chest, opened her dressing gown and looked for a clean towel to spread out between his ear and Jaja's bosom. There wasn't one to be had in the bedroom. He used his own handkerchief.

When he stood upright again, he looked somewhat sour-faced.

'I see.'

'What do you see?'

'She hasn't got long to go! Her heart is worn out. On top of that it is hypertrophied, and her blood pressure is off the scale . . .'

'So how long does she have . . . ?'

'That is a different question . . . If she were one of my patients I'd prescribe complete rest, in the country, with a very strict regime . . .'

'No alcohol, presumably!'

'Especially no alcohol! Complete abstinence!'

'And you'd be able to save her?'

'I didn't say that! Let's just say it might buy her another year . . .'

As he spoke he cocked an ear, because they had both noticed that it had gone very quiet. There was something missing, and that something was Jaja's groans.

When they turned to the bed they saw her, her head raised on one arm, her face set hard, her chest heaving.

She had heard. She had understood. And she seemed to be holding the little doctor responsible for her state.

'Feeling any better?' the doctor asked, just to say something.

But with a suspicious look she lay back down without a word and closed her eyes.

The doctor was unsure whether he was needed any more. He set about sorting his instruments back into his case and he must have been having a conversation with himself, for every now and again he nodded his head in a sign of approval.

'You can go now,' Maigret said when he was ready. 'I suppose there is nothing else to fear?'

'Not immediately, at least . . .'

When he had left, Maigret sat down on a chair at the foot of the bed and filled a pipe, for the pharmaceutical smell was making him feel sick. Likewise, he hid the basin he had used to wash the wound under the wardrobe, not knowing where else to put it. He felt calm and heavy. He looked steadily at Jaja's face, which seemed more swollen than usual. Perhaps that was because her hair, which was swept back, was quite thin and revealed a domed forehead marked by a small scar above the temple.

To the left of the bed, the divan.

Jaja was not asleep. He was sure of that. Her breathing was quite irregular. Her closed eyelashes kept quivering.

What was she thinking about? She knew that he was there, watching her. She knew now that her engine had broken down and that she didn't have long to live.

What was she thinking? What images were there behind that domed forehead?

Then suddenly she sat up, frantic, in a single movement, looked at Maigret with her bewildered eyes and cried out:

'Don't leave me! . . . I'm afraid! . . . Where is he? . . . Where's the little man? . . . I don't want to . . .'

He drew nearer to calm her down, and it was in spite of himself that he said:

'Be quiet, old lady.'

She was indeed old! A poor fat old woman sodden with drink, with her ankles so swollen that she walked like an elephant.

And she must have covered hundreds of kilometres, back home, next to Porte Saint-Martin, continually treading the same stretch of pavement!

She allowed him to lay her head back on the pillow. She can't have been drunk any more. They could hear the police officer downstairs, who had found a bottle and had poured himself a drink, all alone in the back room. Suddenly, craning to hear, she asked anxiously:

'Who is it?'

But other sounds came to her: footsteps in the street, still some way off, then a woman panting, out of breath – for she was running – who asked:

'Why is there no light on in the bar? . . . Is it because . . . ?'

'Shush . . . Don't make so much noise . . .'

Then someone knocking on the shutters. The police officer downstairs going to the door. More sounds in the back room, and finally someone running upstairs.

Jaja was frightened and gave Maigret an anguished look. She almost cried out when she saw him head for the door.

'You two can go!' Maigret said to the police officers as he stepped back to allow Sylvie to come in.

And Sylvie came to a sudden stop in the middle of the

room, her hand on her heart, which was beating too fast. She had forgotten her hat. She didn't understand what was going on. Her eyes were fixed on the bed.

'Jaja . . .'

Downstairs, the first policeman must have been serving the second policeman a drink, because there was a clink of glasses. Then the main door opened and shut. Footsteps were heard heading off in the direction of the harbour.

Maigret made so little noise, so little movement, that it would have been easy to forget that he was there.

'My poor Jaja . . .'

And yet Sylvie did not dash to her side. Something held her back: the glacial look that the old woman fixed on her.

So Sylvie turned to Maigret and stammered:

'Did she . . . ?'

'Did she what?'

'Nothing . . . I don't know . . . What is wrong with her?'

One strange thing: despite the closed door, despite the distance, they could still hear the tick-tock of the alarm clock, so fast, so staccato that it sounded as if it was free-wheeling and about to shatter.

Jaja was approaching a new crisis. A perceptible shudder began to creep through her soft body, firing up her eyes, drying out her throat. But she stiffened. She made an effort to hold herself together, while Sylvie, distraught, not knowing what to do or where to go or even what position to adopt, simply stood in the middle of the room with her head bowed and her hands joined across her chest.

Maigret smoked. He didn't feel impatient any more. He knew that he had closed the circle.

There was no more mystery, there were no more surprises. All the characters in the tale had taken their respective places: the two Martinis, the elder and the younger, in their villa, where they were compiling their inventory with the help of Monsieur Petitfils; Harry Brown at the Provençal, where he calmly awaited the outcome of the investigation while continuing to run his business via telephone and telegraph . . .

Joseph locked up . . .

Now Jaja sat up, at the end of her patience, at breaking point. She looked at Sylvie angrily. She pointed at her with her good hand.

'It's her . . . That poisonous witch . . . That wh—!'

She used the foulest word in her vocabulary. Her eyes pricked with tears.

'I hate her, do you hear me? . . . I hate her . . . It's her . . . She fooled me for ages . . . And do you know what she called me? . . . The *old woman* . . . That's right! Old woman! . . . Me! The one who . . .'

'Lie down, Jaja,' said Maigret. 'You'll make yourself ill . . .'

'Oh! You . . .'

Then suddenly, with a fresh burst of energy:

'But I won't let her! . . . I won't go to Haguenau . . . Do you hear? . . . Or else I'll take her with me . . . I don't want to . . . I don't want to . . .'

Her throat was so dry that she instinctively looked round for something to drink.

'Go and get the bottle!' Maigret told Sylvie.

'But . . . she is already . . .'

'Just go . . .'

He walked over to the window, to check that there was no one in the house across the street. There was no one at the window, at least.

A strip of street with uneven paving stones . . . A street-lamp . . . The sign of the bar opposite . . .

'I know you are protecting her, because she is young . . . Perhaps because she has already made offers to you too . . .'

Sylvie returned, rings around her eyes, looking weary, and handed Maigret a half-full bottle of rum.

And Jaja chuckled:

'I'm allowed a drink, now I'm on my last legs – is that it? I heard what the doctor said . . .'

But just the thought of it put her in turmoil. She was afraid of dying. Her eyes were haggard.

Nevertheless, she took hold of the bottle. She drank, thirstily, watching each of her two companions in turn.

'The old woman's about to pop her clogs! . . . Well, I don't want to! . . . I want her to die before me . . . Because she's . . .'

She suddenly went silent, as if she had lost her train of thought. Maigret didn't move a muscle, merely waited.

'Did she talk? . . . She must have done, otherwise they wouldn't have let her out . . . As for me, I tried to get her released . . . Because it wasn't Joseph who sent me to see the son in Antibes . . . It was me alone . . . Do you understand?'

Yes, of course! Maigret understood everything! He had learned everything he needed to know a good hour earlier.

He made a vague gesture in the direction of the divan.

'It wasn't William who slept there, was it?'

'No, he didn't sleep there! . . . He slept here, in my bed! . . . William was my lover! . . . William came here for me and me alone, and it was she, who I took in out of the goodness of my heart, who slept on the divan . . . Did you not suspect that?'

She yelled all this in a raucous voice. Now it was just a matter of letting her speak. It was coming from deep inside her. It was her true essence, the real Jaja, Jaja naked, that was being exposed to the light.

'The truth is that I loved him and he loved me! . . . He appreciated that it wasn't my fault that I never got a proper education . . . He was happy when he was with me . . . He told me so . . . It pained him to leave . . . And when he came back here he was like a schoolboy at the start of the holidays . . .'

She wept as she spoke, and that made her face adopt a strange grimace that the pink light filtering through the lampshade rendered even more hallucinatory.

Especially as she had one arm strapped up in a piece of apparatus!

'And I didn't suspect a thing! I was stupid! You're always stupid in cases like this! I was the one who invited this girl, who kept her here, because it's always fun to have young people around . . .'

Sylvie didn't move a muscle.

'Look at her! She's still giving me a look! She's always been the same, and I, fat idiot that I am, thought it was just because of shyness . . . I was touched by her . . . When

I think she seduced him wearing my dressing gowns, flaunting everything she had!

'Because it was what she wanted! . . . Her and her pimp Joseph . . . William had money, dammit! . . . And they . . .

'Anyway! The will . . .'

And she grabbed the bottle and glugged down mouthfuls of rum. Sylvie took the opportunity to give Maigret an imploring look. She could hardly stand up. She was wobbling.

'It was here that Joseph stole it . . . I'm not sure when . . . No doubt one evening after a few drinks . . . William had spoken about it . . . And Joseph must have said to himself that the son would pay a good price for this piece of paper . . .'

Maigret was barely listening to this story, predictable as it was. Instead, he looked at the room, the bed, the divan . . .

William and Jaja . . .

And Sylvie on a divan . . .

And poor William must have no doubt compared the two . . .

'I suspected something when I saw Sylvie give William a look one day as she was setting off after lunch . . . I still couldn't believe it . . . But straight afterwards he said he was going to head off himself . . . Normally he never left the house before the evening . . . I didn't say anything . . . I got dressed . . .'

The key scene, one that Maigret had reconstructed long before! Joseph paying a short visit with the will already in his pocket! Sylvie who had got dressed earlier than usual and who had had lunch in her town clothes in order to set off straight afterwards . . .

The look that Jaja spotted . . . She said nothing . . . She ate . . . She drank . . . But no sooner was William out of the door than she pulled an overcoat on over her indoor clothes . . .

No one left in the bar! An empty house! A locked door . . .

They all went off in pursuit of each other . . .

'Do you know where she waited for him? . . . The Hôtel Beauséjour . . . Out in the street I was walking up and down like a madwoman . . . I wanted to knock on the door, to beg Sylvie to give him back to me . . . At the corner of the street there was a knife seller . . . And while they were . . . while they were upstairs, I was looking in the shop window . . . I didn't know what I was doing . . . I felt the pain all over . . . I went inside . . . I bought a flick-knife . . . I think I was probably crying . . .

'Then they came out together . . . William looked completely different, as if rejuvenated . . . He even took Sylvie into a sweet shop and bought her a box of chocolates . . .

'They parted company in front of the garage . . .

'That's when I started running . . . I knew he would be heading back to Antibes . . . I blocked his way, just outside of town . . . It was beginning to get dark . . . He saw me . . . He stopped the car . . .

'And I shouted out:

'"Take this! . . . Take this! . . . This is for you! . . . And this is for her! . . ."'

She fell back on the bed and curled up into a ball, her face bathed in tears and sweat.

'I don't even know how he got away . . . He must have pushed me away, closed the door . . .

'I was all alone in the middle of the road and I was almost run over by a bus . . . I didn't have the knife any more . . . Maybe I left it in the car . . .'

The only detail that Maigret had overlooked: the knife, which William Brown, his eyes already misting over, no doubt had the presence of mind to throw into some bushes!

'I got home late . . .'

'Yes . . . The bars . . .'

'I woke up in my bed, feeling ill . . .'

Then, sitting up, she said again:

'But I won't go to Haguenau! . . . I won't go! . . . You can do whatever you like to make me . . . The doctor said it: I'm going to die . . . And it's this wh—'

There was the sound of a chair scraping across the floor. Sylvie had pulled a seat towards her and collapsed on to it, sideways on.

She passed out slowly, gradually, but it wasn't feigned. Her nostrils were pinched, ringed with yellow. Her eye sockets were hollow.

'It serves her right!' Jaja cried. 'Leave her! . . . Or maybe not . . . I don't know . . . Maybe Joseph organized everything . . . Sylvie! . . . My little Sylvie . . .'

Maigret leaned over the young woman. He tapped her hands, her cheeks.

He saw Jaja grab the bottle and take another drink, literally pumping alcohol down her throat, which caused her to cough violently.

Then the fat doll sighed and buried her head in the pillow.

Maigret took Sylvie in his arms, carried her down to the ground floor and dampened her temples with cool water.

The first thing she said when she opened her eyes was:

'It's not true . . .'

Deep, total despair.

'I want you to know that it's not true . . . I don't try to make out I'm better than I am . . . But it's not true . . . I love Jaja! . . . He was the one who . . . Do you understand? . . . He was making eyes at me for months . . . He begged me . . . How could I refuse, given that I did it every evening with strangers . . . ?'

'Shush! Not so loud . . .'

'Let her hear me! If she thought about it, she would understand . . . I didn't even want to say anything to Joseph, in case he took advantage . . . I arranged to meet him . . .'

'Just once?'

'Just once . . . You see! . . . It's true that he bought me chocolates . . . He was besotted . . . So much so that he frightened me . . . He treated me like a young girl . . .'

'Is that all?'

'I didn't know that it was Jaja who . . . No! I swear! I thought it was Joseph . . . I was afraid . . . He told me that I should return to the Beauséjour, where someone would give me some money . . .'

And, in a whisper:

'What could I do?'

They heard a moan from upstairs – the same moan as earlier.

'Is she very seriously injured?'

Maigret shrugged his shoulders, went upstairs, saw that Jaja was sleeping and that she had been moaning in her unconscious state.

He came back downstairs and found Sylvie, who was a bag of nerves, jumping at every sound in the house.

'She's asleep!' he whispered. 'Shush . . .'

Sylvie didn't understand and looked at Maigret with an expression of dread; he merely filled a pipe.

'Stay by her side . . . When she wakes up, tell her that I have left . . . for good . . .'

'But . . .'

'Tell her that she was dreaming, that she was having nightmares, that . . .'

'But . . . I don't understand . . . And Joseph?'

She looked into his eyes. He had his hands in his pockets. He took out the twenty banknotes, which were still there.

'Do you love him?'

She replied:

'You know full well that I need a man! Otherwise . . .'

'And William?'

'That was different . . . He was from another world . . . He . . .'

Maigret walked to the door. He turned round one last time, as he fiddled with the key in the lock.

'See to it that we don't have to talk about the Liberty Bar again . . . Do you understand?'

The door was open to the cold air outside. The ground was exhaling a damp vapour that was like a fog.

'I didn't think that you were like that . . .' Sylvie

stammered, not knowing what to say. 'I . . . Jaja . . . I swear she is the best woman in the world . . .'

He turned round, shrugged his shoulders and set off in the direction of the harbour, stopping a little further along under a streetlamp to relight his pipe.

11. *A Love Story*

Maigret unfolded his legs, looked the other man in the eyes and handed him a stamped sheet of paper.

'May I?' asked Harry Brown with an anxious glance to the door, behind which were his secretary and his typist.

'It's yours.'

'I want you to know that I am prepared to give them compensation . . . A hundred thousand francs each, for example . . . Do you understand? . . . It is not a question of money: it's all about the scandal . . . If those four women were to come back home and . . .'

'I understand.'

Outside the window could be seen the beach of Juan-les-Pins, a hundred people in swimsuits lying on the sand, three young women doing physical exercises with a long, thin instructor and an Algerian who went from group to group with a basket of peanuts.

'Do you think a hundred thousand would . . . ?'

'I'm sure, yes!' said Maigret, standing up.

'You haven't had your drink.'

'No, thank you.'

And Harry Brown, so correct, so well groomed, hesitated a moment before hazarding:

'You see, inspector, I thought for a while that you were the enemy . . . In France . . .'

'Quite . . .'

Maigret headed for the door. Brown followed him, sounding less sure of himself:

'. . . scandal isn't as big a deal as it is in . . .'

'Goodbye, monsieur!'

And Maigret bowed slightly, without offering his hand, and left the suite and all its busy wool trading.

'In France . . . In France . . .' the inspector muttered as he descended the purple-carpeted staircase.

In France what? What would you call Harry Brown's liaison with the widow or divorcee in Cap Ferrat?

A love story!

So what about the story of William, with Jaja, with Sylvie?

Maigret had to weave his way between semi-naked bodies as he walked along the beach. The brightly coloured swimsuits showed off the bronzed flesh to its best advantage.

Boutigues was waiting for him next to the physical education instructor's hut.

'Well?'

'Case closed! . . . William Brown was killed by an unknown assailant who wanted to steal his wallet . . .'

'But . . .'

'But what? . . . No dramas! . . . So . . . ?'

'Yes, but . . .'

'No dramas!' Maigret repeated as he looked at the blue sea, calm as a millpond, and the canoes paddling about. Was there room here for dramas?

'Do you see that woman in the green swimming-costume?'

'She has very thin legs.'

'Exactly!' Boutigues cried out in triumph. 'You'd never guess that she is . . . Morrow's daughter.'

'Morrow?'

'The diamond merchant . . . One of those dozen or so people rich enough to . . .'

The sun was hot. Maigret in his dark suit stood out among all this bare flesh. Snatches of music could be heard coming from the terrace of the casino.

'Would you like a drink?'

Boutigues was wearing a light-grey suit and had a red carnation in his buttonhole.

'I did tell you that round these parts . . .'

'Yes . . . These parts . . .'

'Don't you like it here?'

And with a lyrical sweep of the arm he indicated the extraordinary blue of the bay and its huddle of white villas among the greenery, the yellow casino like a cream bun, the palm trees along the promenade . . .

'The large man you can see over there in the small striped swimsuit is a top German press baron . . .'

And Maigret, his eyes a dull grey after a sleepless night, muttered:

'So what?'

'Are you pleased that I made you *morue à la crème*?'

'I can't tell you how much!'

Boulevard Richard-Lenoir. Maigret's apartment. A window opening on to some scrawny chestnut trees with as yet only a smattering of leaves.

'So what was the story this time?'

'A love story! But, as they told me: *No dramas . . .*'

His elbows resting on the table, he ate his salt cod gratin hungrily. He spoke with his mouth full.

'An Australian who had had enough of Australia and all those sheep . . .'

'I don't understand.'

'An Australian who wanted to live it up a bit, so he did . . .'

'And then?'

'Then? . . . Nothing! . . . He went and did it, and his wife, his sons and his brother-in-law cut him off . . .'

'That's not terribly interesting!'

'Not at all! I told you . . . He continued to live down there, on the Côte d'Azur . . .'

'I've heard it's lovely down there . . .'

'Magnificent! . . . He rented a villa . . . Then, as he was on his own, he found himself a woman . . .'

'Now I'm beginning to understand!'

'That's what you think . . . Pass me the sauce . . . Not enough onions.'

'They're Parisian onions, completely tasteless . . . I put a pound of them in . . . But go on . . .'

'The woman moved into the villa and brought her mother with her . . .'

'Her mother?'

'Yes . . . However, the charm of that arrangement soon wore off, and the Australian went to look for some fun elsewhere . . .'

'He took a mistress?'

'But he already had one! And her mother. He discovered a bar and a good woman to drink with . . .'

'She drank?'

'Yes! After a few drinks, they saw the world differently . . . They were at the centre of it . . . They told each other stories . . .'

'And then?'

'The old woman thought it had finally happened to her.'

'That what had happened?'

'That someone loved her . . . That she had found a kindred soul . . . And all that . . . !'

'And all what?'

'Nothing . . . They were a couple! A couple of the same age . . . A couple who liked to get drunk as they . . .'

'What happened?'

'There was a little protégée . . . Her name was Sylvie . . . The old man became infatuated with Sylvie . . .'

Madame Maigret gave her husband a reproachful look.

'Are you pulling my leg?'

'It's the truth! He became infatuated with Sylvie, and Sylvie didn't want to, because of the old woman . . . Then she must have wanted to, because, after all, the Australian was the main character.'

'I don't follow you.'

'It doesn't matter . . . The Australian and the young woman ended up in a hotel . . .'

'They cheated on the old woman?'

'Indeed! You see, you are following! So the old woman, realizing that she didn't matter to him at all any more, killed her lover . . . This cod is superb . . .'

'I still don't get it . . .'

'What don't you get?'

'Why didn't you arrest the old woman? After all, she did . . .'

'She did nothing!'

'What do you mean, "nothing"?'

'Pass me the dish . . . They told me: *Best if you avoid any dramas* . . . Don't make waves, in other words! Because the Australian's son and wife and her brother-in-law are very important people . . . People who are able to pay top dollar for a will.'

'Now what's this will you're on about all of a sudden?'

'Let's not make it more complicated . . . In short, it's a love story . . . An old woman who kills her old lover because he's cheating on her with a young woman.'

'What happened to them?'

'The old woman has only three or four months to live, depending on how much she drinks . . .'

'How much she drinks?'

'Yes . . . Because she has a drink problem . . .'

'It's very complicated!'

'More than you know! The old woman, the killer, will die in three or four months, maybe five or six, with her legs swollen and her feet in a tub.'

'In a tub?'

'Yes. It's how you die of dropsy, according to the medical dictionary . . .'

'And the young woman?'

'She is even more unfortunate . . . Because she loves the old woman like a mother . . . And then because she loves her pimp . . .'

'Her what? I really don't understand you . . . You have such an odd way of expressing yourself . . .'

'And the pimp will blow the whole twenty thousand francs at the races!' Maigret went on regardless, without stopping eating.

'What twenty thousand francs?'

'It doesn't matter!'

'I'm completely lost!'

'Me too . . . Or rather, I understand too much . . . They told me: *No dramas* . . . So that's it! . . . We won't mention it again . . . A little love story that turned out badly . . .'

Then suddenly he said:

'No vegetables?'

'I wanted to make cauliflower, but . . .'

And Maigret paraphrased to himself:

'Jaja wanted to make love, but . . .'

OTHER TITLES IN THE SERIES

THE FLEMISH HOUSE
GEORGES SIMENON

*'She wasn't an ordinary supplicant. She didn't lower her eyes.
There was nothing humble about her bearing. She spoke frankly,
looking straight ahead, as if to claim what was rightfully hers.*

*"If you don't agree to look at our case, my parents and I will be lost,
and it will be the most hateful miscarriage of justice . . ."'*

Maigret is asked to the windswept, rainy border town of Givet by
a young woman desperate to clear her family of murder. But their
well-kept house, the sleepy community and its raging river all hide
their own mysteries.

Translated by Shaun Whiteside

INSPECTOR MAIGRET

OTHER TITLES IN THE SERIES

THE MADMAN OF BERGERAC
GEORGES SIMENON

*'He recalled his travelling companion's agitated sleep – was it really sleep?
– his sighs and his sobbing.*

Then two dangling legs, the patent leather shoes and hand-knitted socks.'

A distressed passenger leaps off a night train and vanishes into the woods. Maigret, on his way to a well-earned break in the Dordogne, is soon plunged into the pursuit of a madman, hiding amongst the seemingly respectable citizens of Bergerac.

Translated by Ros Schwartz

INSPECTOR MAIGRET

OTHER TITLES IN THE SERIES

And more to follow